Sanitarium Magazine
Issue no. 39

Thank you to all of our contributors, we couldn't have done it without you.

FACULTY MEMBERS

Dr. Sputnik
Dr. Muratori
Dr. Soldan
Dr Algee
Dr. Marceau
Dr. Warra

Contents

ISSUE THIRTY-NINE

Dear Reader,

When people become aware that I work in the horror industry the questions are normally the same, we have even covered this in a previous post on the website. However, this month with the events that have played out on our screens, news feeds and airwaves have made me reply to the age-old question "why do you like horror?" My answer is "because it isn't real, once you close the book or the credits start to roll it's over and it can't get you."

Sadly, for those caught up in these awful events, it is all too real and the true monsters have shown how evil mankind can be. (Even if it just s tiny, tiny subset of it).

So my thoughts are will all victims of the cruel acts of terrorism and I hope an end comes swiftly to it.

Barry Skelhorn

Vandals In The Repository by Peter Hynes

Of COURSE, HUNTER LED THEM DOWN the desiccated stairways, past dimness into dark, his tall body one contiguous, always flexed muscle. Varlet was next in line, flashlight skirmishing with the black. Wren kept her hand inches from his back, as though afraid he would step too far beyond the circle of light and disappear.

The hallway crumbled like sunburned skin and coated them with its castoffs. Fiona started coughing. "Dammit, Hunter," she wracked. "You couldn't have brought whatever it is to us?"

Hunter halted before a door. Opened it. "Over there," he said, and the group allied their flashlights to reveal the object there.

"You cannot be serious," Varlet said.

The body was cat, a panther, crouched as though surveying a field crowded with prey. The head was incongruous - too large, too equine - and crested with a forearm length horn.

Hyper scurried closer, cradling his hammer. Fiona crouched here, there, humming softly in appreciation, camera clicking, flash strobing. Varlet rubbed a tentative hand over the stone, like he expected static shock. The statue showed no sign of a creator, no lines of chisel, no edge of imperfection. "Amazing. Like it was made for us to transform it."

Wren jolted from her study. "Varlet, are you sure?"

"Very sure." In the tepid light Varlet's smile was a clenched fist with white knuckles. He scanned the company, receiving its anticipation, feeling its destructive energy. "Have at it," he said.

Hyper, predictably, stepped up first. The statue resisted his hammer, defied his grunting impacts. Fiona snickered even while dancing around the arc of the sledge. Hyper's agitation finally made him swipe petulantly at the one piece that seemed vulnerable: the horn. It leapt from the chiselled snout and penetrated the floor, an inverted stalagmite. Encouraged by his unexpected victory, Hyper whirled his hammer like some shrunken Thor and severed the beast's head.

The rest joined in, sweat lubricating the stone as they struck sparks from it. The statue was soon exquisite ruin. A treasury of portent and revelation, if only they knew how to read the jumbled pieces.

***

The building had been a hospital. Now, it sat segregated from the surrounding blocks, littered with detritus of its past life, such as glassless radiology shields and rusting examination tables. Paint curled into scales. Halls led into tall, desolate wards. The floors echoed with long-past panicked transports. In the week since discovery, Wren had muralled the entire pigeon-infested cafeteria with depictions of sundered bodies and derelict lives, and the structure had been dubbed the 'Repository'. Their storehouse of effects deemed essential: gas lanterns and heater, CD player, batteries, CDs. And their tools, the hammers, axe, crowbars, spray-paint. Their means of bringing order to its knees, and putting one to the base of its skull.

Dusk dragged the day's remaining light from the room. Some sort of convalescent ward, spider-frame beds stacked in one corner like a hurried barrier against intruders. Varlet told Hunter to light the lamps. Hyper tacked thick blankets across any glassless windows. Wren pouted. She liked the colours of sunset. "Like God cut his finger on the moon," she murmured.

The space was bricky and rough, bare and cold. The gas heater's warm spokes held the group in place, as guttering lantern light peeled and remade their faces. Wren fingered her piercings, comforted by the cool solidity. Varlet signalled for a beer, which Hyper reluctantly provided. The room was silent but for burbling sips, the rut-like slap of blanket against concrete as wind probed entry, and the lantern's drafty hiss.

Fiona wandered over, camera dangling from one sullen shoulder. She squatted beside Hunter, lit a cigarette. Fiona. Jeans, silk collar and knee-high boots. Rich-daddied prima-donna wandering the city wastelands, rooting out derelicts and pain-freaks to acquire via her lens. Obsessed with image, especially her own.

She watched Hyper unravel a beer can with pliers, finding him amusing, like a hungry puppy. Hyper, hair a wiry explosion, eyes unable to fix on anything for long, glanced at Fiona, nearly slicing off a finger in distraction. He held up the peeled tin and grinned. Fiona rolled her eyes.

Varlet leaned into the lamplight, shadows hardening already strong angles. Wren recalled a bonfire on the cement roof, with Varlet clutching Fiona's thin hips as they swayed to a Nick Cave song of murder-most-foul. Wren went to ask Hunter to dance. Her own hips did not feel so thick beneath his huge hands. She watched Fiona photograph Varlet, who lit a smoke, drawing long before inserting it in Fiona's mouth. "Which the hook, which the bait?" Wren asked no one.

And wondered about their recent find downstairs.

The plan had been for another fire, with Hunter sent in search of fuel, usually collapsed crates or abandoned furniture. He had returned with a cumbersome pile of combustibles and news of something to show them. The statue.

Her recollection was interrupted when Hyper blurted to his feet, called, "I'm going rambling," and returned to the door leading downstairs.

"Boy just can't get enough," Hunter said.

Hyper danced down a shaky staircase, oblivious to its instability, until he hooked a foot on a hole near the bottom. The flashlight clattered ahead and his palms bruised on the floor. Spritely back to his feet, tossing damp hair into position, he breathed, "Fine." And set to punishing the stairs with his hammer.

He savoured the jolting recoil. When the bottom half-dozen stairs were suitably abstract, he retrieved the flashlight and set off down the corridor, sweeping the hammer from side to side. He might have to settle for punching his code into these walls tonight.

At the end was a door solid as a shotgun stock and fit like a shell in the chamber. He hoped it had no lock. He would never live to beat it in.

But the handle turned, and the door floated inward. His light extended far enough to decide the dark had it outnumbered. Never one to focus on the perfectly relevant, Hyper then wondered why the old floorboards did not creak beneath the obvious weight of whatever was now treading them.

He was halfway up the hall when the horn staked its claim on him.

Wren watched Varlet study a volume of macabre art, stripped of several layers of inky skin by constant perusal. The page showed a forest of broken-boned flora, ornamented with nightmare foetuses, open-bottomed, like visceraless hand puppets. Slip up into me, they seemed to urge. Tell me what to say, where to look. Wren believed any hand inserted into them would soon be lost. "You going to turn the page?" she asked. He had not noticed her peering over his shoulder. "Here," he said. "Enjoy."

Wren accepted the book, but it was the sharing of its secrets she sought, not solitary impression. She could sense Fiona's smirk without seeing it. Hopefully, she would wander off soon to snap pictures, maybe even fall down a hole. "Late, like the rabbit," she muttered before thinking to catch herself.

She ignored Fiona's finger-round-the-temple bit. She had seen it before.

Instead, she hummed through the CDs, seeking something to match the unformed song vibrating the steel pin in her lip. Varlet nodded approval as Swans grumbled out of the stereo.

Wren pulled aside a window-blanket and watched the wind flay trees. Her nipple rings pressed into her skin and she felt like squeezing them to a sharper bite. She thought about their numerous 'projects'. Covering walls of schools, factories, welfare offices with discordant designs; making homes of crumbling, castoff structures; venting themselves of frustrations upon the inanimate. Things considered worthy of creation and then abandoned when deemed flawed or no longer useful. Like their parents, teachers, gods had done.

She surveyed a wide wall, and set to designing a new mural. Her dead brother, perhaps, his tiny body choked blue by a man brought home to sate some need of mother's. And, eventually, to feed on them all.

Hyper's "Don't touch me!" jerked her about. He was striding away from the door and a freshly rejected Fiona, arms wrapped around his chest as though trying to keep his heart from escaping. Fiona shrugged at their inquisitive glances, a 'hell with him' look on her face. Varlet walked to Hyper, who crouched with clenched eyes and forsaken solace.

"Hey, man," Varlet said, squatting a few feet away.

"Get away from me."

"Can't do that, pal. You take a fall, or something?"

Hyper laughed. He sounded like a poisoned man reaching for a cigarette and remembering he had quit. Hunter wandered over to offer a beer. "Here, little man. Chug-a-lug."

Hyper took the can and swallowed without opening his eyes. When he did, they fixed on Varlet. "Too big to be that fast," he breathed.

"What? Is someone down there?" Varlet stood and looked at Hunter, who started for the door, grabbing an axe that looked like a hatchet in his grasp.

"No!" Hyper jumped to his feet. Groaned. "Shit, man, it felt real." He surveyed the squints and perplexity around him. "The beast, you morons. The statue, it stampeded me downstairs." He bunched his shirtfront in a shaking hand. "It impaled me, man." His eyes begged Varlet for an explanation. Hunter snorted. Fiona threw a disgusted look at the trembling boy, adding, "Asshole."

Varlet stood. Hands entered pockets. "The statue."

"It was real!" He buried his face in his arms. "Hurt like real," he moaned.

"And where is it now?"

Hyper's shoulders answered, 'Who knows'?

Varlet nodded, weighed Hyper's demeanor. "Hunter," he decided. "You take point."

Hyper held his protests, with both fists.

***

The room that held their gear was also the intersection point of several routes of descent. Varlet and Hunter considered their options.

"Follow the path of damage," said Hunter.

Varlet agreed. "Hansel had his breadcrumbs, Hyper his hammer. You will dissuade any mobile sculpture that tries to run me through, right?"

"Of course."

Onto a stairwell, where the walls resembled lunar photos. It was no feat to follow Hyper's progress. At the bottom was an open door. Hunter stepped in, following the room's left-hand wall. Varlet followed. "Point your flash up," Hunter said.

Varlet complied and saw a tangle of thin bones descending upon him. Hunter grabbed him before he hit the floor. "Careful. It isn't going to hurt you."

Varlet shrugged him off, eyes on the statue. As he moved his flashlight's beam from bottom to top, the sculpture's form resolved: a tree, the clustered branches atop the mistaken skeleton. Its edges fled the flash's beam. Varlet decided that this tree would have never given up its knowledge of good or evil.

"So, you going to play Paul Bunyan now?" Hunter sized up the stone figure and nodded. Varlet stood back. "All right, you axe-toting maniac. Let's see your swing."

The first blow rebounded. The axe recoiled and landed away into the dark. Varlet spared his friend the pressing laughter. "Oh, dear," he said. "Hurt your hands?"

"Bite me." Axe retrieved; Hunter studied the trunk. Undamaged.

Not a leaf fallen. He glanced at Varlet's outline behind the flashlight.

"Come on, big man," the outline said. "Uproot the damned thing and let's go."

Hunter stiffened, then smiled. <u>Roots.</u> Foundation, balance, foothold. He dropped down, knelt, the floor hard and soft at once like scraped flesh, like a scab and, sure enough, hooked in were spiny fingers, the roots. Hunter stood, twisted to exclude his feet as targets and swung. No sparks, no recoil, no chipping grunt of nicked stone. Meat.

He circled the base, severing the stone where it entered the floor. Varlet wondered what artist strove for this level of realism and left his creation to starve in the depths of a deserted hulk. But there perhaps was the point - that artist wished it left unanalysed. Hunter advised, "Step back," leaned a shoulder to the trunk, and set his weight to the graven bulk.

***

Wren had broken out her chalk and was scrawling contorted mayhem across the floor. Colors like a blind man imagines; blueprints for the head trip your parents' religion played on you. When the boys returned, she offered Hunter a glance, enough to note his sweat and grin. Varlet waved to her. Smiled at Fiona.

Wren hunted for her purple, the one with the streaks of blue in it. Hyper shuffled over to watch. "That's what it felt like," he said softly, rubbing his chest, pointing at the mural.

Wren believed him.

"So, lads," Fiona called. "Did you slay the stone beast?" Hunter and Varlet traded looks; some fading subtext visible.

"Found Hyper's trail," Varlet said. "Way he was swinging that mallet, be a miracle anything survived to find."

"Poor boy. Looks down to see a huge horn, no wonder he got scared." Fiona laughed. "For sure it had to be imaginary."

Hyper cleared Wren's drawing in one leap, Fiona's face free of surprise when he took her to the concrete, to whatever kept her from falling away, from escaping before he could pluck that smirk and suck its bitterness to nothing on his tongue.

She was smiling. Pulled up her shirt with a free hand, the outhills of her breasts revealing - not nipples, those were still pink, still alive - these patches were dead. Burns, Hyper's mind gagged. Scars. She was still smiling.

"Been done by better than you, horn boy. And liked it more, too." Hyper slid away from her, oblivious to Hunter's proximity, to how close he had come to being tossed away. "Bitch," Hyper said.

"Let it go, man," Hunter whispered. Wren ignored them all. And started another mural. It would be something dead.

***

The lamp was fading for want of fuel, yet they ignored it. Hyper sat too close, greasy forelock glistening. Fiona watched him and laughed quietly - see the silly monkey, should we pet him, feed him? Varlet offered no protest. Wren sat on the concrete, drawing an autopsied child, chalked first in moist health, then stripped of afterbirth, flesh, viscera. She watched her hand reveal new detail before her mind could catch up. Wishing the others would contribute. Fiona, got what she desired by playing dangerous while mommy and daddy were off keeping up appearances. Hyper was mere hooligan. Varlet would smile and wander off to invent new ways of sticking it to the bourgeoisie. Hunter, perhaps, would have something to offer, if only appreciation.

And then he was there. He squatted, knowing the intimidation of his height, and studied the innocent dissection. "You're quite the interior decorator," Hunter said.

Wren laughed. "Just rearranging the furniture." She sifted through her chalk for the right shade of necrotic grey. "What really went on down there?" she asked.

He watched her hands, envious, for his own were tactless. "I'm going for blankets," he said, noting her shiver. As he walked away, he turned and said, "You see a lot more than the rest of us."

Wren studied the drawing beneath her knees, wisped away stray chalk. She supposed it was what he meant.

***

Hunter descended the two flights to the storage room, wondering if there might be some food left to be scored with the blankets. And about Wren.

He had heard Varlet grant admiration for her eyes and their ability to transform, depict, discern. But there was too much of her there for Varlet. Those eyes were shielded in pudgy flesh, her jaw like she had just returned from some unpleasantry at the dentist. Hunter saw the bond she tried to forge, and Varlet's obliviousness. Too blinkered by Fiona. Could the petulant masochist, with her see-right-through-me figure and thieving camera, be such a superior find? Wren redesigned reality with her chalk and ink. Fiona just stole it from others and put it on display.

He went to the steamer trunk they had found in a blazed-out house months before. Popped the twin latches, claimed the blankets within, then dropped the cover into place. As he stood straight, the trunk withered into a gross seed, and the shadows turned to thicket.

He tried to step away. A bass drum beat in his chest, the echoes rebounding off the inside of his skull. A copse of agitated tree trunks appeared. His legs turned scabrous, skin-broken, pain. His feet slipped into the floor, now dirt and mulch, toes stretched like time while waiting for an axe to fall to the neck. Nuts burst from his fingers, pain, his skin crumbling in a November wind. Pink flesh petrified, became bark, sap-stuck and peeled. Pain.

About, towers of trees made of flesh, but gray-rotted and seeping pus. Something scurried through his hair, down a stiffened arm, screeching flight. Away. A beast crashed on heavy feet through a nearby thicket. A hot wind arrived, set him swaying. Just before he saw the sweeping sunset glow approaching. Just before the burning began.

***

When he woke, taut and joint-locked on the concrete floor, it was several minutes before he remembered anything but smoke, flame and withering limbs.

A face parted the haze of recall. Hunter struggled to stand, fighting the urge to curl back into a huddle. Varlet spoke to another figure, something about drink. Hunter finally reached his feet. The beer cleared a dream of soot from his throat, as he panned the room and found concern wrapped in shock. They had never seen him weakened, forget helpless.

"I'm alright."

"The hell." Fiona stepped into the lantern light. "You were choking when we got here." His head was full of A forest aflame, terrified animals blurs of retreat, feet gripped by ground, skin smouldering. And correlations. A horned beast goring its persecutor. A stone tree visiting ashen irony upon the one to brazenly fell it. Hunter now knew that fire did not burn. It chewed.

"We have to leave."

"Have to?" Varlet.

"The statues. They..." He looked at Hyper, who had jumped and clutched his chest. "Those things are more than they seem. That tree I took down paid me back in full."

"You had another nightmare. Like Hyper?" Wren.

Hunter smiled. "I enjoy my nightmares, little one. This was experience. Beyond any you could have in this world."

"Like 3-D?" Fiona.

"Like dying and getting called out of your tomb, shutterbug." Varlet walked to the window, studying the moon like a familiar face he must put a name to. The others shuffled and muttered about Hunter's solo demolition of another statue. Deciding they really did not resent being left out, after all, thanks much. A circle formed about the lantern.

"Okay." Wren said. "I say we find out what's going on."

Varlet sighed. "Pack the gear."

Wren crossed her arms. "You lost your balls pretty fast." Varlet considered her reflection in the window. The cracked glass split her from the rest, projection of her dissent. "Go explore then, little Wren. I'll not risk any more of us."

"Risk what?" she snorted. "Bad dreams?"

Varlet whirled. "Look at him." Pointing at Hunter. "You know him as well as I do. Look. And talk some more about 'bad dreams'." Wren skulked a glance at Hunter. Unable to voice her disgust at their cowardice in the face of something so powerful and intent.

Hyper terrified. Hunter weak and shrunken. What artist could have fortified its creations with such power?

"I'm going downstairs," she said.

Varlet watched her for bluff. The rest stalled their evacuation.

Watching the tug-of-war.

"Shit," Varlet muttered.

***

Varlet, hissing lantern in hand, trying to regain face by taking the lead. Wren behind him. Hunter brought up the rear. Varlet stopped and turned. Hyper's continued march peeled Fiona's shoes from her heels, getting him an elbow to the windpipe. The silence thickened. Feet scuffed further dust into the air.

"Aren't we a jolly band," Hyper mumbled, rubbing his throat.

"Aren't we just." Hunter's first words since leaving the meeting room.

Down another flight, resolve eroding, dark nipping, backs vulnerable. They had roamed tight night spaces before, worked in crystalline quiet, listening for official footfalls, raised voices. The dark must always be carried, but this was inert. This dark was dead weight.

Then, an open door. Varlet's lantern made little more than an indentation, revealing nothing but a few feet more of dusty floor. He hesitated. Listening.

"Well?" Wren sighed. "Waiting for an invitation?"

"Jesus, Wren, what do you want?" Hyper pushed past Fiona. "We looked, okay? Our honour is intact. Now, can we go find something to smash and start laughing again? Please?"

Fiona scuffed dust. "I thought you knew, boy. Pincushion's not big on laughter."

Varlet nodded. "We leave." Even in the scattered light relief was evident. My god, Wren thought, back to breaking windows and calling it art. Hunter returned to the hall's closed entrance and grabbed the handle. Confusion and then frustration worked

20

into his face. He slammed a shoulder into the door twice, cursed, and turned to face the group.

"I guess we're going forward."

Huddled as tightly as the doorframe would allow, they stepped into the dark room ahead. Flashlights and lantern painted the area and, a dozen strides in, found occupants.

Hyper yelped and stumbled into Wren. Hunter's shoulders slumped then rose, anger finally cauterizing what would not be healed. Fiona handed the lamp to Varlet and fumbled at her lens cap.

The statues were assembled as though for marching orders. A narrow path ran down the centre, twin columns of shadowy stone to each side. Wren started down that avenue. Hunter moved in front of her. She smiled at his protectiveness. "Think you could demolish them all?"

"Be a lot of bad dreams, Wren."

"Should we try?"

"If you'd been where I have, you wouldn't ask."

Wren turned. "I know you. You've an axe in your mind matching the one in your hand." Hunter examined the figure on his left. A mermaid, but no fisherman's love. An eyeless, jut-boned face, a body full of scales sharp as the insights of your nemesis, tendril-length fingers, waiting to return to lightless depths and find the drowned, to aid the ocean in stripping their bones. "I wouldn't know how to fight that," he said. "None of us would."

Wren studied the mermaid, remembering every nightmare of drowning, of rising to a surface that raced away faster, while air kicked at flimsy lungs that hungered, even for the water. She smiled at its strength and nodded. "Let's find the exit."

Hunter grabbed Hyper's elbow and coaxed him forward. Wren was studying an altar, bare but for three spikes on its top. The nails must have been carved from the same piece, yet it seemed they might roll off if the pulpit were tipped. She gestured ahead. "I think Varlet's up there."

Hyper nodded. "Then that's where I'll be."

They rebanded at the room's far end, where Fiona held the lamp on a seam in the wall behind more statues. The one in front was a clown blowing into a balloon that was a child's screaming face. Behind the clown a stone rose bush blocked the door. Each thorn had a cross-stem shaped like a sharpened crucifix. "If we move this one," Varlet tapped the clown, "we should be able to chop open the top half of the door."

"Hell, yeah." Hyper said. "Doors I can do."

They grabbed the excuse to laugh. Even Fiona had a smile for him. Varlet and Hunter sought handholds. "Keep the lights off that damned face," Hunter said. None asked which. "Ready?" Varlet asked.

"On three." Hunter crouched, grip firm.

"Three."

The clown was oblivious to their efforts. The statue slid away from Hunter's hands, as though offended by the formality. He fell, colliding with more stone, stone that mocked his graceless tumble and bruised his skull. He rolled, head full of chisels and mad sculptors.

Wren pushed her way between statues, squatting to cradle Hunter's head. Her light in his eyes, he cursed and she moved it.

"Slowly," Wren cautioned.

He made his knees and leaned his head back. Then frowned, and looked again over Wren's shoulder. "We're not getting out of here," he said.

She tried to grasp Hunter's sudden pessimism, would not have thought it possible to bring that expression of resigned defeat to his face. So she looked behind her. Hyper's face grinned in the light, pale and static. It was another statue, and it was one of them.

"Varlet," she called. "Bring the lantern over here."

In the fuller light, the statue was revealed. Hyper, frozen, but fighting the stone restraint. The hands were sledgehammer heads. The face was dented, pocked with impacts. From the chest protruded at least a foot of stone horn. They silently appraised it, avoiding the flesh counterpart beside them. Hyper took in the replica, looking as though he had been slapped by his shadow. "Move away," he said.

They moved aside. Hyper ran a finger the length of the horn, his chest a breath from its tip. It seemed to struggle for release, as if sensing the proximity of flesh. "Just shadows," someone whispered. Hyper shook his head. "No." And severed the horn from the statue at its point of exit.

They let him be, his expenditure a comfort. Something familiar, something understood. The statue grew into a brittle pile. Pieces shifted, settled and stilled. Hyper watched for more movement, breath slowing enough to reveal sobs piggybacking it. He slapped at a tear. Wren moved closer, unreadable eyes on the mound of rubble. Hyper looked past her. And snarled.

Hunter pulled Wren away. Hyper's hammer just missed her skull. Sobbing, scrambling, Hyper leapt atop the carved flowers. The long thorns pierced his shoes, raising the pitch of his cries but sparing his resolve. Blood coloured stone roses. Sparks and clamour filled the space. He swung at the door, the kickback almost pitching him off the statue, yet he was bound, anchored by the crucifixes impaling his feet. Varlet called for him to stop. Hunter stepped forward, grunting as the hammer's shaft struck his shoulder. He gripped it and wrapped an arm about Hyper's waist. His efforts ended, the boy finally felt the spiked fetters in his feet, and screamed. Tossing the hammer aside, Hunter murmured apology and pulled Hyper from his perch.

At the spatter of blood on the floor, Hunter had his coat off and wrapped around Hyper's stricken soles. His legs pistoned and pulsed. Hunter took a foot in the chest but held his place. Hyper's thrashes weakened, his eyes unsure what they were looking for. Then, they closed and moans replaced the screams. "Not a mark on it," Fiona said.

"What?"

"The door. Not a nick taken out." Varlet spat and ground out curses.

"He's shivering." Hunter was holding Hyper's head. "I've already given up my coat." Eyeing Fiona. But Varlet had his off and laid it across the still gently jerking form. "It's stone, too," he said. "So good it looks like wood, but it's stone."

Hunter stood. "The statues all had a weakness." Fiona considered this. "No knob. What about hinges?"

Varlet jabbed a finger at her. "Yeah. Toss me a light." He guided the flash along both edges of the door. Sighed another curse. "If there are any, they're on the other side."

"Great." Fiona moved closer, arms coddling her torso. "We're going to be our own final project. We destroy ourselves and become part of the decay."

Varlet summoned Hunter. "If we can't find a way out," he handed Hunter the sledge, "then we'll make one." And moved into the hall.

Wren listened to their pounding determination as she sat between Hyper and the rubble of his stone twin. She tugged at her rings, forcing sensation. Fiona strolled the floor, watching the dimly lit assault in the hall outside and said, "Just had to have your adventure, hm?"

Wren twisted a ring harder. "I didn't have my hand on your leash."

"No, just on Varlet's ego. He's supposed to look out for our interests, not join in your treasure hunts."

"Our interest was in finding out what the hell happened to Hyper and Hunter."

"So, do we know now?"

Wren looked up, looked hard. "You can go to hell anytime you like."

"Newsflash, pincushion," Fiona said. "The trip's been made." Wren nestled her chin between her kneecaps, arms around her calves. Fiona lit a smoke and wandered away to inspect the others' progress. Not impressive, according to the curses and frustrated grunts to be heard.

Wren sifted through the pile of shattered statuary, delving until she found a piece of the face. Hyper's eye, cheek, split grin. She looked up as Varlet stalked into the lantern light and threw a hammer on the floor. Hunter followed with the axe. Its handle was broken a foot from the head.

"No luck?" Wren.

"Please." He waved at the wounded axe. "The door's the same as the one Hyper went ten rounds with, and behind all that plaster is just another abundance of stone."

They gathered around the door. Wren sat by the wrecked statue, brought a fragment closer, looked into its lone eye. Hunter lingered, seeking as well the knot that held it all together. He pictured the dissected baby made so real by Wren's chalk and smiled. "Well, little one. Think you can draw us a door that'll lead out of here?"

Wren felt the edge of the stone cheek still in her hand. "Maybe," she said, "the destruction is just the first step. Maybe we weren't changing. Just preparing."

Hunter studied her eyes. "Maybe we're what's being prepared." Wren opened her mouth, response undecided, then nodded.

"Maybe," she whispered, then turned to Hyper and he whimpered. The company huddled about him. Their concerns fled as Hyper, punctured soles scraping the floor, opened his eyes and let loose the sound of a lunatic breaking the last whole piece of his mind.

The circle broke. They stepped, slid, staggered backwards. Hunter wrapped a restraining arm about Fiona. Her struggles fit the rhythm of Hyper's howling. Hunter kicked aside bits of broken statue, seeking a way to access the space about the boy, whose limbs lashed as though he were caught in a swarm of unseen wasps.

And he was carved.

Hyper stiffened, stretched, plunged into a foetal ball, arms wrapping about his legs, bones straining, joints popping, his flesh flayed, rent, slid from his face in leathery pages. His legs drew tighter, his chest opened to allow them access, his screams ended as the others began, even Hunter shouted frustrated, sickened grief. Wren paced around the lip of the light-circle, eyes wide, and Hyper's antics ended as he was tucked into a tighter ball, then pulled oval, his own skin wrapping inside-out, sheathing him in a soft glistening shroud. The shape was modified, as further sculpting proceeded across what had been his back. His spine was smoothed of vertebral roughness before flesh covered it. Fiona hung limp in Varlet's arms, back to his heaving chest. Sticky, congealing detritus seeped across the floor from what had been Hyper.

The form sat unmoving before them. Their companion's body had been expertly transformed into a glistening, fleshy egg.

From one section near the top was a jagged opening, like beak-pecked shell. From it protruded the one remnant of humanity. A plaintive hand.

Fiona heard it first - stone sliding along the floor. Her legs ended their marathon and she fell, her mouth licked tears and, "Oh god, one of the statues is moving...", and she slid back to Varlet, wrapping herself around him.

The other two burst away from the sound, Hunter in front, reflex defender. He surveyed the room with a flashlight and whispered, "Damn." He stepped forward to confirm. "Not a statue, shutterbug," he said. "The door opened."

***

Hunter, as always, went first. The others followed closely to stay within the influence of the lantern he held. Wren wondered at Hyper's reconstruction, and whether she could ever have depicted such a thing herself. Dead foetuses were nothing.

The new room was confining after the space just left. It smelled dank and sour. The light flickered over the walls like flame across fresh paint. The company's remaining members were solemn, taut, breathless, studious. Pondering the meaning of the display before them. Varlet wrapped an arm about Fiona. Hunter craned the light towards the centre and panned across the still figures there. Wren kept her mind on the shattered remains outside, of Hyper and his likeness, trying to pick up the thought-thread severed by their comrade's butcherous transformation. Something, there had been something...

The statues were life-size, each approximated the height of its model. Four pieces, four faces. Four petrified nightmares.

Hunter: strong face wrenched in agony, peering from the barky trunk, rooted in its own cremation, the tree of his torso withered, limbs burned to twigs.

Varlet: expressionless as he dangled from a gibbet made of women's legs, arms, smooth backs. The noose his own aroused, elongated member, straining at its burden as it choked his air.

Fiona: fossilized, graceless wings stretching from her shoulder blades, bones like a fabric fan, each pinned to a backboard of stone. A devolved butterfly mounted for examination.

Wren: in a skeletal embrace, forged Siamese with some faceless, unknowable figure. Impossible to discern where she ended and her partner began, a snapshot pose of lovers caught in the flash of some nuclear event, some captivating heat.

Fiona sank to the floor. Varlet followed, supporting her descent. Hunter turned to ask after Wren, but found only empty space. He scouted the room, methodically patching each fracture in his once wrought-iron composure. A gritty shuffling came from the larger storeroom.

"Wren?' She was just outside, her butane lighter on the floor before her, squinting in its anaemic illumination. Hunter stood in the doorway, watching the lantern light glint off of her piercings. Fiona shrieked protest from within.

"Dammit, Hunter, where are you going with that light?" Varlet yelled. Hunter positioned the lantern between the rooms, trying to make out what Wren was doing. "Wren is out here alone."

"Well, that's up to her. You keep that lantern on us." Varlet shone with sweat, and Hunter could not tell how much of the trembling was being transferred from Fiona. "She wants to wander in the dark, that's damn well up to her."

"Tell the little bitch to stay put," Fiona moaned into Varlet's shoulder.

Wren remained focused on her task. Hunter handed her one of the nearby flashlights. She shook it off, so he rolled it into the adjoining room. She had several pieces of Hyper's statue in hand, touching them together, turning them to seek a better fit. Wren felt the edge of the stone cheek she held. Soft, like clay. She tumbled the stone pile apart and pulled the other eye from the heap. She reintroduced it to the first piece. It stayed.

"The destruction," she said, heart kicking at her breath, "is just the first step."

Hunter crouched beside her. She quickly had a stone arm near completion. "Look." She held the finished face before him. It was free of rents and pits. The skin was smooth, the expression contemplative. Hunter sighed.

"Hand me a piece," he said.

Hunter watched Wren meld pieces into wholes, yet his own efforts did nothing but grate dust from the shards. Only when Wren guided his hands, found the grooves just so, did they adhere for him, with no scar of former injury. A torso rose, unsteady on one leg, then firmly on two. He heard murmurs from the other room, then footsteps. Varlet and Fiona appeared in the doorway.

"What the hell..?" Varlet said, as Fiona lurched from his grip and landed on Wren, fists swinging, eyes wide. Hunter grabbed at her. "Stupid whore," Fiona spat. "You made us come down here and now you're going to make it worse and we're all going to wind up like him," as she wrenched Wren's head towards the bloody egg that had been Hyper, as her foot found the legs Wren had built and toppled the carving to the floor. A limb broke off and rolled.

Hunter found his grip and pulled. Fiona hung, hair striking, heels drumming. Varlet stepped towards Hunter. Wren began searching for fitting pieces again.

Varlet turned on her, wrenching her arm. "Are you insane?" Wren stared into him. "Do you see? How they meld together?

Can your pretentious little gigolo's mind grasp the fact that we're supposed to reassemble what we destroy? That we're not getting out of here unless we replace it?" She glanced at what Hyper had become. "We're clay, Varlet. Unless we prove otherwise."

He stood, a hand still gripping her arm, but thinking. Surveyed the pieces, Wren's interrupted work. Fiona found her breath.

"Jesus, Varlet, are you going to listen to her? Who knows what this thing wants, now she's messing with this statue again, and look what happened to Hyper when he..."

"Well, that's up to me to chance, isn't it?" Wren snapped. "The hell it is, freak. You want to piss in this psycho-sculptor's pool, you do it when the rest of us are gone."

"Enough," Hunter growled. He dropped Fiona to the floor and moved between her and Wren. He looked at Varlet. "It's all we've got, man."

Varlet spit on the shattered bits at his feet. "Leave it the hell alone while I think."

He stalked off into the adjoining room, Fiona at his back, one wary eye a farewell to Wren. She grabbed the lantern and was gone.

Hunter crouched, found the lighter and flicked it into life again. Wren sat, head in hands, angry flush on her cheeks. "I was only..."

"I know."

He watched her join two more of the shattered pieces. His eyes left to chase a thought, but it was broken when, from the next room, a new sound arrived.

Varlet screaming.

Hunter turned to the door; the wail joined by disbelieving sobs from Fiona. Varlet was quickly silent, as Fiona's moans turned to agony and Hunter went to the doorway and stopped, looked back. "Wren..."

She was already into the pile, the leg reattached, a skull fragment fitted, an ear found, and Hunter found the hammer, moved toward the door, more strenuously prompting, "Wren," and she couldn't get the elbow to fit, had to turn it over, and she wanted to tell him not to go, but she needed to find the hand, the right hand, it was here, she had seen it...

A grunt left the room, a solid, stubborn admittance of pain, and the words that followed spoke of a violently emptied womb, or the cry of a genocide's last survivor being buried by his own people's dead hands...

She had an arm completed. The chest. A shoulder. Her hands found the correlations; her eyes wandered the growing torso looking for gaps.

Something was being peeled beyond the dark doorway. Something was becoming something else, something that had been someone. The statue's arms were fastened, settled comfortably. Head met stony neck, Wren ground it in, willing it to adhere. Fighting the need to look behind her, through that doorway. To see the bloody art she knew sat softly drying there. She heard Hunter groan, and she turned, he held the hammerhead before him and, voice demanding, he asked, "Can't you control it?"

But how to control such brutal expression? Rein in a sculptor for whom even flesh was more material? Dark beauty that spoke of violations and grief and the bastard had come to her room that night, that same night her brother died and she had wanted to change him, make him something useful, give him purpose other than to inflict, like this old hospital, useless and dank yet full of potential, echoing pain, mortality, change...

Clay. Putty. Stone.

Wren's hand slipped, a piece of statue fell, as a correction rose from some valley of her mind. Not sculptor. Sculptress. She looked at Hunter, who still peered into the adjoining room. She scanned the statues, no longer blind to her signature. And was proud.

"Wren," Hunter said, voice rusty, "however, whatever, you have to stop." He moved toward her, the hammer in his hand gaining altitude. His wide back to the room become bloody studio, the only sound now hard breathing.

Her gaze moved to him. "All my life," she said, "I've been trying to change or improve or reveal. All. My. Life. I think..." She met his eyes. "I think that the only way to control this is to stop wanting it. And I do want it."

Wren sat in a flickering shield of light, dim stone shapes all about. She rose and stepped away, lighter held high. The statue of Hyper - reformed, serene, now missing the stone horn that had protruded from its chest - stared back at her. It was smiling.

"You're the only one who ever tried to see." Wren's hands, now taskless, began to tremble with exertion and excitement. "All artists need to learn discipline, I admit it. But now that I know, now that I'm aware, Hunter, just think. All the users and petty people, all the selfish shits, they can be made beautiful metaphors. Oh, Hunter. The world a museum. Think of it."

Hunter squeezed the handle. The hammer stayed raised. "Please, Hunter." Wren fixed her eyes on his. "You don't have to be afraid. You understand."

"And what happens when you run out of material?" he whispered.

Wren sighed as the hammer's head bolted towards her own. "I can only hope," she said, "to live long enough to find out."

***

The sculptress wandered her studio, spent perfunctory time cleaning up after herself. Working certain materials was untidy. She pondered the bloody sculptures still drying, ignored their stone counterparts, their models. The glistening hanged man and skeletal butterfly. A particular one she approached, noting its bony limbs, the strength of its trunk. She ran a hand across its charred, fleshy bark. Appropriate, a worthy representation of his strength, of the preparation and replenishing that fire brought for new growth. But she did wish a little that he had appreciated her work. She could enjoy training an apprentice. There were, after all, so very few worth instructing.

The End.

CASE #41069

VANDALS IN THE REPOSITORY
BY PETER HYNES

"Peter Hynes is a native Newfoundlander, split-brained and indecisive enough to have completed half degrees in both French and Business. He presently pushes pencils for a security firm, and writes fiction on his lunch breaks. His stories have appeared in such publications as Flesh & Blood, Transversions, The Malahat Review, On Spec, Dark Tales, Wicked Hollow, and Aiofe's Kiss."

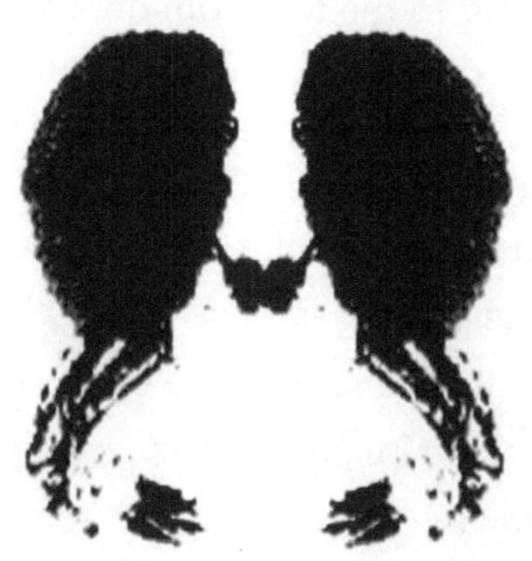

The Needle's Eye by Thomas Staples

Miles tipped back the cup, taking a swig of coffee. As it fell into his mouth, he winced, not at the heat, but at the taste. He always avoided going to the tea room on a Tuesday, as this was when the short haired brunette was there working her shift, she never made it correctly. It was surprising she wasn't fired weeks ago.

Thursday was the day for Miles. The woman who was behind the counter then knew what she was doing. Miles wasn't sure if he found her more attractive than the other one, or if it was just her coffee making skills he admired so greatly. But today was a Thursday and it tasted off. She hadn't seemed her usual self either. Miles was used to the pleasant greetings and the occasional flirt, but not today. Today was different, today was wrong.

Miles looked across the table, where his long-time friend Stephen Harris sat.

'Burnt your lip, again?' asked Stephen. 'Not quite' said Miles, chuckling. 'What is it then?'

'This tastes bloody awful.'

Stephen didn't believe him, and decided to try himself. He reacted to it somewhat dramatically, like he was hoping someone would notice and get it replaced. They didn't.

'Yeah, you're right. Not up to the standards of Thursday Girl at all' he said with a sour look on his face.

Miles laughed at this, neither of them actually knew her name. He looked across the crowded room, over the bald heads and clattering of cutlery to where she stood, her face blank and expressionless as she took the daily orders. Miles turned back to Stephen and idly stirred his coffee, using the cheap wooden stick they provided so woefully.

'How are things with...?' Stephen paused '...Bear?'

'Jesus, Stephen. Do we have to keep calling her that?' replied Miles.

'Yeah, it's a codename. She spends lots of time outdoors, so does Bear Grylls. Therefore we call her-'

'I know' interrupted Miles, 'but do we need a codename at all?' 'Of course we do, so we can talk about it in public without people catching on, like in high school' Stephen said with enthusiasm. 'I'm twenty-six.'

'Exactly!' replied Stephen, having another sip of the coffee as if the taste had gone away, it hadn't.

Miles chuckled, and did the same. The taste settled a little, but it was still awful.

'I might just go and get us two teas' he said, standing up.

'You aren't getting away that easily, Mister, sit!' replied Stephen, pointing to his chair.

Miles complied, reluctantly.

'"Bear" is fine, good in fact. I'm heading over tonight' said Miles.

'Oooh, when should I join you?' joked Stephen.

'Very funny' replied Miles, smiling.

'But hey, if it doesn't work out, you can always settle for me' Stephen smiled back.

'I might take you up on that. Right, back in a minute'

Miles stood up and walked over to the counter, the queue was non-existent. He waited d near the cash register, while Thursday Girl was nowhere to be seen. He stretched over the counter to see where she was, and spotted her standing near the coffee machine with her back to him.

'Excuse me' he said, politely.

She didn't respond, she just kept staring blankly. If only Miles knew her name.

'Excuse me' he repeated, louder this time.

Her head twisted around to face him, the body lagging behind. She looked at him--No--*through* him, as she walked towards Miles, perfectly silent.

'Just two teas, please' asked Miles.

Acknowledging this, she pushed several buttons on the register, displaying a number on the screen.

'Two ten' said the woman, her words as blank as her face. Miles fumbled around with the change in his pocket, pulling out two pounds and twenty pence. He handed it over. As she looked down to count it, Miles spotted something strange. The looseness of her shirt revealing the skin around her neck.

Somewhere between the thyroid and jugular was a thick black mark, running around her neck and out of sight. It made Miles feel uneasy, and somewhat afraid. His head quickly jolted into an upright position when he realised she was done counting.

She held out a ten pence coin in her hand. Miles plucked it carefully, avoiding any contact with her skin. She walked away for a few minutes, before returning with two teas and placing them down on the counter. The pale liquid spilling over the rim of the cup and settling in the saucer. Miles grabbed them and walked back to his table, where he sat down.

'Cheers' said Stephen, whose head was buried deep in the daily newspaper.

'I didn't know Thursday Girl has a tattoo' said Miles. 'Huh… Neither did I. What kind?'

'Like… One of those take autopsy things that people have. Y'know, one that makes you look like you've been stitched up?'

'I didn't realise people actually had them' said Stephen, taking little interest. 'Whereabouts?'

'Around her neck' replied Miles.

'Interesting place to have it, I guess it'd look pretty creepy' *Oh, you have no idea*, thought Miles.

'Well, after that insight, let's drink up' said Stephen, his eyes locked to the paper. '*A Farewell to Famine*' Stephen spouted, 'you hear that Miles? You can stop being a vegetarian now.'

'Nice try' replied Miles, with a smile. 'The writer must have been a Hemingway fan. What does it say?'

Stephen didn't get it, so he pretended to laugh.

'Meat is back on the menu, baby!' he exclaimed. 'Bloody sick of eating vegetables, but their reign of terror is finally over!'

'I'm very happy for you' said Miles, as he necked his tea. 'Now, off to do… Whatever it is we do'

'I second that' said Stephen, as he finished his.

The two of them had a much better time with the tea, although it tasted a little weak, they weren't going to complain after the coffee travesty.

The pair of them stood up and left, leaving their dirty cups and empty sugar packets behind. The newspaper sat open on the next page, the picture showed a woman sitting in hospital with tears streaming from her eyes, and a caption saying *Birth Failure Fiasco Continues*.

Miles and Stephen went back to their shifts of sitting in a dark warehouse away from civilization, hammering away at their keyboards until the day was over. Miles barely knew what his job was, he just had to respond to emails, take pictures of kids' toys, and answer phone calls from customers who had a "complaint". *"Is your child dying? No! Has the new model of Optimus Prime become self-aware? No! Now get off your ass and do some damn parenting"*

Miles had always wanted to say that, but in the interest of being able to afford his rent, he kept it to himself. Despite it all, Miles couldn't shake that sight from earlier. Thursday Girl's tattoo, the image of it bounced around in his head like a flexible bullet, sending the occasional shiver down his spine. It was so vivid, so detailed… So real.

Miles stood in-front of the mirror in his bathroom, ruffling his dark, puffy hair until it looked how he wanted it to. He scrubbed his teeth, feeling the sting of the toothpaste on his gums. His teeth were yellowed at the sides, while the ones that took centre stage were much whiter. He spat into the sink, ignoring the slight splatter of blood that game with it.

He threw on his jacket and looked at the clock. *8.23pm* it displayed. It was pitch black outside, the light from the streetlamps filling the streets with a weak bronze layer.

Miles left his apartment, locking the door behind him and heading down the steps into the street below. It was cold, bitterly cold. Miles was shivering even with the extra layers. *At least it's not too far,* he thought.

Miles walked up the street, passing by all the lit-up houses, feeling envious of their heat. He stuffed his hands in his pockets, it didn't help. He pulled his jacket tighter to him, that didn't help either. He kept strolling until he reached the park in the centre of town. *I'll cut through, that'll save time,* which was the worst idea that Miles had that night.

The park was well maintained, the grass kept flat and vibrant. The benches were cleaned and replaced whenever they began to deteriorate, and the paths were shown the same amount of care. Miles climbed over the gate, and proceeded onto the path ahead. It was much darker now, there were only four lights up the stretch of concrete.

He could just about see the fountain in the distance, and he remembered something horrific about it. There had been cases of people tripping and hitting their heads on the edges of the stone fountain, where they busted their head open and died. It had happened on three separate occasions, which resulted in the new

"No Climbing on the Fountain" sign. It was unsettling to look at, so Miles kept walking.

He could see the house in the distance, the house that belonged to the woman they referred to as "bear", or "Jen" as Miles would call her (Seeing as that was her name). Miles smiled to himself at the thought of this. But his smile soon faded, when he saw *him*.

At the furthest light up the path was a man. He stood under the strong beam of light, not flinching, not shivering. Miles saw that the man was naked, his arms down by his sides without a care in the world. Then he saw something else, something horrific. The man had a mark going across his chest, a thick black mark. It came down from both of his shoulders and met in the middle of his chest. Miles couldn't fool himself into not believing what he saw, because it was as clear as day. That wasn't a mark, or a tattoo… It was a stitch.

As Miles' legs carried him unwillingly closer and closer to the man, the image became clearer. The dark red scarring that ran across his body, the blooded clips that were embedded in his flesh, and the tight red string that looped through his pierced skin, pulling it together. When Miles became aware, he was still walking, he stopped dead. Maybe the man hadn't seen him? Not possible. He was looking right at Miles. No--*through* him.

For a short while, nothing happened. Miles' brain was coping with what it was going to do next. The two of them stood about fifteen feet from each other, until the other man began to close the gap. He started walking towards Miles, dragging his bare feet across the ground, his arms still slumped down by his sides. Miles remained frozen, his body not wanting to run away, or to fight. All it wanted to do was wait, and hope it all blew over.

The man got closer.

Miles put his right foot in-front of his left, and vice versa. It was like he'd never walked before and was now just learning. His heart hammered away in his chest, the blood and oxygen pumping around his body faster and faster.

The man got closer…

Miles walked faster and faster, he wanted to get past this man and just continue with his evening.

And the man got closer.

They were within spitting distance, Miles stood to the man's left, avoiding all eye contact. As he passed by him, he saw something he'd never want to remember, he even fooled himself into thinking it would be possible to forget. The man's mouth was curved upwards at the sides. His entire body lacked any emotion, his face was blank, except for that cold smile. He didn't look drunk, or high. He looked… dead.

They began walking away from each other, like they didn't notice one another in the slightest. As the distance increased, Miles' felt his heart slow down, it was no longer trying to punch its way out of his chest. The gut-wrenching fear that welled within his stomach had subsided, and he carried on.

Look behind you, Miles thought, *make sure he's gone.* Miles didn't comply, he kept walking until he'd reached the final light on the pathway, where he'd first seen the stitched-up man. He unclenched his fists and relaxed. Only then did he do what his brain told him to.

He turned around.

Miles could still see the man in the distance, not as clearly as before, but clear enough to be certain of one thing. He was coming towards him, and this time… he was running. Miles ran too, not focusing on anything other than getting out of there. The light faded as he left the streetlamps behind. He did what you should never do, he turned around again. The man was coming for him, and soon he would catch him. Miles kept his balance faced forward again, the gate was within reach.

He reached the end of park and clambered over the fence. Taking less care than before he scraped his leg and fell onto the other side, rolling into the street. He scrambled to his feet and kept running as fast as he could through the dimly-lit street. He saw Jen's house and ran straight for it. Hopping over the stone wall, he hammered on the door with his fists as hard as he could. Going against his better judgement, he turned around one final time.

The stitched-up man was nowhere to be seen. As the door swung open, he dashed inside and slammed the door behind him. The sound of his own heavy breathing blocking out what the woman who answered was saying. He knew it was her and that it was safe now. As sweat poured from his chalky pale skin, Miles felt everything fade into darkness, as he lost consciousness and collapsed.

***

The kettle clicked, Jen poured the hot water into a cup and stirred. Miles liked his coffee a certain way, and it didn't take her long to pick up on this. Once it was made she carried it over to him. Miles was sat in her living room, his hands gripped tightly onto the armrest of the cream-coloured sofa.

'Here, just how you like it' said Jen, handing the cup to Miles. 'I never told you how I liked it' replied Miles, the fear in his voice was still present.

'I learned' she said, cracking a smile and sitting beside him. Miles didn't smile back, instead he stared into his coffee and thought of her. Thursday Girl, and the mark around her neck. It had seemed so real at the time, and now Miles knew why. He took a large sip of coffee, oblivious to the heat which should have burned him. He sat quietly and thought. About the girl, about the man, not knowing what to say about any of it. Eventually, Jen broke the silence.

'Are you going to tell me what happened, Miles?' she asked.

'I was chased here' he said, pausing to think. 'I was chased here by a man, probably coked up out of his mind.'

The flood gates had been opened, and the lies poured in. It is one thing to think you might be losing it, but it's another to have everyone else thinking the same. Besides, he found Jen to be incredibly attractive. As much as he refused to admit it, he wasn't always thinking with his brain, and this was one of those times.

'It just really spooked me, y'know?' continued Miles.

'I can imagine' said Jen.

'When I turned around, I saw him just walking away, like nothing had happened.'

Jen was relieved, as was Miles. Nothing like a successfully crafted lie to raise spirits. Miles finished his coffee and took it into the kitchen. He placed it on the worktop and washed his hands. He felt Jen's breath on the back of his neck before she placed her arms around him. Miles flinched at this, enough for Jen to notice.

'Oh shit, sorry. I didn't-' said Jen, aware of what she'd done. Miles turned around and pulled her closer for a kiss, cutting her off. The two of them stood there in the kitchen, before Jen pulled away, smiled at Miles and headed upstairs. He waited for a few moments before heading up after her.

Once the two of them were finished, Jen drifted off to sleep. Miles was still wide awake. Despite the intimacy that took place, his mind was on other things. He was frightened to overlook her naked body in case he saw the dreaded stitching, but in the darkness he couldn't see clearly enough. *She's not trying to kill me so that's a good sign,* thought Miles.

Miles checked his phone, the time was *11:45pm.* The battery was low, very low. He looked to his left and saw a cabinet with a lamp on it. Resting on the cabinet was also a charger. He sat up and tried plugging it in. After several stabs in the dark there was an audible *click,* the phone lit up briefly, letting Miles know that it was charging. *I'm sure she won't mind,* he thought. Out of the corner of his eye, he saw that the window blind wasn't completely down.

Look out the window…

It was the same voice that told him to look behind him in the park. So he did. He stood up and edged over to the window. The blind was pulled, letting a tiny amount of light in. He lifted the bottom with his hand, carefully, to make as little noise as possible. Light leaked in through the window as he did so. He kept lifting the blind, wanting to see more.

Miles could now see out across the street, but more importantly, he could see the park. It was empty. No stitched-up man, nothing but darkness with the odd streetlamp polluting it. Miles' mind was just playing tricks on him, maybe it had been this whole time. At least he thought it was, until he looked down.

Standing on the curb directly ahead of Miles was a man, a naked man. A man who was covered in stitches, across his shoulders and chest. A man who was still smiling… He glared up at Miles, who did little else but glare back. The man spoke. Miles couldn't hear what he said, but the mouth movement was enough to figure it out.

"Let me in"

This sent a chill down Miles' spine. The fear in his stomach had returned and was throttling it remorselessly.

"Let me in"

'No' whispered Miles.

The man tilted his head questioningly, before looking down. He began to walk towards the front door. Miles stepped back and let the blind clatter against the windowsill. There was a loud crash as the man thumped on the door with his fist, it rang through the house. Then another, and another. Jen sat up erratically and threw on her clothes. Miles did the same, before flicking the light switch on.

'What the bloody hell was that?' said Jen, looking at Miles.

He was paler than earlier, like all of his blood had made one final ditch effort to get away from the man, not caring about the body that needed it. Miles stared blankly at the wall, his mouth open and eyes bulging.

'Miles?' she asked, he sensed the anger in her voice.

'It's him' he said, turning to face Jen.

'The man from earlier?'

'Yeah' he replied, his words dying on their way out of his mouth. 'This may sound crazy but…'

'What is it?' asked Jen.

'His body is--He's all stitched up. Like he's been cut open and sewn back together'

'Stitches?' said Jen, tilting her head questioningly.

'Yes, and I saw someone earlier today with them. Right around their neck', he did actions to compliment this.

Miles was no longer facing Jen. The crashing had stopped momentarily, but it was barely missed with the pounding of his heart.

'Stitches…'she repeated.

'Yes!' said Miles, turning to face Jen once again.

'Like these?'

Jen held her shirt up, and there they were. Several layers of stitching across her chest and over her shoulders. Miles was struck with fear at her terrifying appearance, she didn't look quite alive, or quite dead. It didn't hit him that the crashing had started again. His eyes bulged out of his skull, they seemed just as eager to get the hell out of there as the rest of him did. But Miles did nothing except look back across Jen's face, and when he did, he saw what he'd never wanted to see again that day. That big… stupid… grin…

***

Stephen was zoned out in his apartment staring at the most recent episode of… What? He didn't even know. He barely paid attention to it, he was too drunk out of his mind to give a damn about anything. In hindsight, that was probably the point. He checked his phone, *11:45pm*. Before he placed it down, he saw it tick over to the next minute.

I bet Miles is having an interesting night, Stephen thought to himself.

Oh, you have no idea.

Stephen picked up the glass that rested on his recently purchased copy of *A Farewell to Arms*, it was empty. He turned to his right and found the bottle was empty too. *Great*, he thought. Then he remembered, the shop down the road on the corner was open 24 hours, they sold decent booze. He thought about heading to bed, but he wasn't drunk enough for that yet. He intended to wake up the next morning with the meanest hangover possible. He'd be waking up with more than that.

Stephen threw on his coat and left the apartment, locking the door behind him. The street was almost pitch black, the streetlamp had been blown out a few weeks ago and the council hadn't got around to replacing it. *I swear to Christ, I will climb up there and fix the bastard myself,* thought Stephen. It wasn't enough of a journey to warrant taking the car, so he left it.

He began to walk down the street, ignoring the lone bark of a stray dog that echoed in the distance. The brightness of the shop ahead felt welcoming in the darkness. The giant *OPEN* sign in red letters was pleasing, yet it stung his eyes the closer he got, he squinted at it until he got inside.

Once inside, the temperature didn't change much. The smell of disinfectant and other harsh chemicals made their way into Stephen's nose and throat. It smelt awful, it tasted even worse. At the end of the aisle was the drinks section. The overpriced wines littered the shelves, most of them being brands Stephen had never heard of. He wasn't interested in the wines, and certainly not in the bottle of Tequila he found. That reminded him of a joke he heard as a kid.

"Why did the Mexican throw his wife off the cliff?" "Because she cheated on him". Stephen never got that joke, why didn't the Mexican just dump her? Maybe he was just horribly misinformed about the punchline.

He saw a bottle of whiskey with the label half torn off and the yellow price tag that degraded to nothing. But it displayed an alcohol percentage of 46 and that was the only selling point that mattered to Stephen. He grabbed a bottle and carried it over to the till where a man was waiting.

'Just this please, mate' he said, placing the bottle down.

The man scanned it, smiling as he did so, and told him how much it would cost.

'Twenty-three, seventy-four.' said the man.

Stephen took his wallet out and fumbled a few notes and coins around, eventually handing over a twenty and a five. The man took the money, and messed around with the till until he produced some change. When Stephen picked up the change, he felt the man's cold skin. It took him by surprise and caused him to flinch.

'Everything okay?' he asked.

'Y-Yes, fine' replied Stephen, trying his best to muster a smile back at the man.

'Have a nice evening' said the man, his mouth curved sharply upwards.

Stephen's smile quickly disintegrated as he left the shop with his bottle clutched closely to his chest. Once he got outside, he paused and let out a heavy sigh. *He had one of them bloody tattoos as well*, thought Stephen, *nearly frightened the shite out of me*. Except this wasn't a tattoo, and Miles would have known this. Going straight up the centre of the man's arm was nothing of the sort, it was a jagged line of stitching. The clips clearly piercing the skin and keeping it loosely together. Stephen shuddered at the thought, before walking back down the street towards his house.

That cursed dog was barking again, this time it seemed closer. Before Stephen had gotten completely out of the light the barking stopped and he heard the light pitter-patter of feet. He looked down and saw the dog sitting in-front of him, it's tailing wagging merrily, dribble lightly coating its chin. Its fur was a golden colour, quite clearly a retriever. Stephen crouched down and ran his hand through its fur. He looked around the dog's neck and saw what appeared to be an incredibly tight collar or at least where one had been. He tried to touch it, and found it was completely absent of fur. Instead, there was a circle of stitches.

Stephen rose to his feet slowly, not taking his eyes of the dog for a second. It stood up as well, and carried on strolling. The pitter-patter of feet getting quieter until it disappeared into the distance.

'Dogs aren't known for having tattoos' said Stephen, a thought that seemed too ridiculous to keep inside of his head.

Stephen started walking again, faster than before, much faster. The light through the window of his apartment wasn't as welcoming as the one at the corner shop, but it was enough to feel like safety. And right now, that was what Stephen wanted more than anything. Then came the coughing and spluttering. Not Stephen's, but that of another man. He turned to his right. The noise was loud, the noise was close. Stephen saw a black outline of a person, slumped over in a heap and sitting against the wall. He took his phone from his pocket, and switched the flashlight on.

The power of the LED light burst forward and the shadow revealed itself. Sat with his back against the wall was a lone man, blood spraying from his mouth as he coughed again and again. He was wheezing between breaths, trying to gather the energy to say something, but he couldn't. Instead, he just sat there, his shirt soaked through with blood, his chest poking out with a bump.

'Jesus...' said Stephen 'what happened to you?'

The man didn't reply, he just sat there, his head tilted to the side. 'I'll call an ambulance, let's get your shirt off' said Stephen, peeling the sticky shirt away from his skin.

The man raised his arms slightly, allowing Stephen to remove the shirt without too much hassle. He threw it aside and looked towards the injured man again. The word injured was quite the understatement, as what Stephen saw next made the muscles in his throat tighten. It wasn't just a basic stomach injury like a knife wound or even a bullet hole. Instead, his entire chest had been ripped open. The skin was separated in three different flaps, each had metal clips piercing the skin, the string hanging down loosely from them after it failed to keep it all contained. The man's chest wasn't poking out because he had a bit of a belly on him, it was just the insides trying to make an exit. And for the most part, they had succeeded. The bundle of intestines had freed itself, drooping downwards in a big pile. Some of the organs were cut up, while others were missing entirely. The ribcage remained intact, but there was something else, something that shouldn't have been there. A small metal plate.

Stephen didn't get a closer look; he couldn't bear to. It was disgusting, it was horrifying, and it was real. He looked up towards the man and backed away. His head rotated slowly in the direction of Stephen, before his eyes locked onto him, his mouth curved at the edges into a terrifying smile.

Stephen ran for it, his apartment wasn't far, he could make it. He'd completely forgotten about the bottle of whiskey, or that he was even still holding it. The light of his apartment got brighter as he dashed for the door.

He reached it, holding the bottle in his left hand and searching for his keys in his right. Just as he found them, his bottle of whiskey smashed on the floor spraying overpriced liquor everywhere. Within moments, Stephen hit the floor too. He'd only had a second to register the freezing cold hands around his neck, but by then it was too late.

***

Stephen's eyes opened slowly, letting the light in a little at a time. He felt a searing pain across his entire chest as he awoke, like he'd been crushed by his own weight as he lay face down on the solid metal table. While the room he was in was dark, the open doorway lead into a corridor that had an unbearably potent light opposite.

Stephen sat up, his head ringing, his eyes squinting at the sight of it. He instinctively put his hands over his face to cover it, the pain being almost unbearable. *This is worse than the usual hangover*, he thought to himself. It was. It was much worse.

He rose to his feet and gained his balance, looking around as he did so. He saw a table. It looked rusted and overused. He then looked down at himself, he was still wearing the same clothes. There was a stain across his shirt from when he dropped the whiskey. He ran his hand across it, it felt dry. He turned back to face the doorway and the light that pierced through it, before quickly shielding his eyes once more. As Stephen made his way through the doorway, he fumbled for his phone and keys, finding both of them. *10:39am* was the time displayed on his phone, and the *27th of November* was the date. He hadn't lost that many hours, no more than the usual. The light from his phone burned through his skull, so he put it away, realising it'd be of little use.

He was now in the middle of the corridor. He looked to the right and saw that it reached a dead-end, and then to the left, seeing that it split into several more corridors. He chose left, and with a great deal of caution, he crept forward. The light from that one lamp only carried him so far as it faded away just as the corner shop's light had.

He got to the end of the corridor, and slowly reached out with his hand. The sudden contact of the wooden door handle startled him enough for him to flinch, the quiet gasp made only louder by the emptiness of the surrounding area. He twisted it and pushed, the door swinging open at his command. The sight he was met with froze him where he stood.

In-front of him was another room, considerably larger and well-lit than his. In the centre was a metal table, much cleaner than the one Stephen awoke on. Laying on this table was a woman. Her chest had been completely cut open and peeled backwards. The pattern was specific, like the cross in the skin of a jacket potato. Surrounding her body were medical tools, blooded medical tools. The woman lying there looked at peace, her hands down by her sides, a big smile upon her face.

'Jesus, fuck' said Stephen, as he staggered to the side, colliding with a medical trolley.

There was a sudden clatter as some of the tools fell from the trolley onto the floor, the sound cutting through Stephen's skull like butter.

'Shit' whispered Stephen.

He heard a clonk, the clonk of giant footsteps storming towards him. It got louder, and Stephen knew precisely what this meant. It was getting closer. He stood as quietly as he could in the darkness as a figure approached the table and looked directly towards Stephen. It was another woman; her clothes were stained through and through with blood. The blue plastic gloves were no longer that colour. In her hands was a round metallic object, a metal plate. She looked down at the table and reached inside the woman's chest, there was a click, and she removed them again. The object was gone, and it was obvious where.

'Brilliant, isn't it?' she said.

Stephen didn't know how to react. He didn't want to speak immediately in case she wasn't talking to him. But deep down, he knew she was.

'Are you still there?' she asked, barely being able to see Stephen in the dark.

Stephen said nothing.

'I know you are, you might as well talk to me' she said, impatiently.

'What... is all this?' replied Stephen, getting the words out after several attempts.

'Lunch' she said, laughing.

'What the fuck?' he said back, the fear in his voice overwhelming it.

'Well, we all have to eat something' 'I don't...'

'In the simplest of terms, my friend, you've been eating people.'

Stephen said nothing.

'Blimey, use your noggin.'

'You kill people, and cook them' he said.

'Not quite, close though. We don't kill them; we just take what we need.' She replied, grinning 'Do you even know how many parts go to waste inside a human body?'

'No, I don't' said Stephen.

'*We* can take one of your lungs, and still you'll keep on trucking. *We* can take one of your kidneys, no problems at all. *We* can take your spleen, your muscle, *we* can even take your stomach, and you'll still keep going.'

'What about the colon?' Stephen asked.

'Sure, that too. If you fancy shitting into a bag that is' she replied, fond of her own joke.

'Why not just kill them?'

'Well, there have been some deaths. It was my fault; I got a bit greedy. It could have screwed the whole thing, but the fountain above made a great scapegoat.'

'What about the ones who are stitched up? They don't function properly anymore. There are people falling apart in the streets!'

'Granted... There were the odd couple of glitches to begin with, but it's fixed now. Apart from the smiling and their tendency to be a tad aggressive. The more recent ones are none the wiser that it's even happened to them.'

He reached out for the medical trolley, grabbing the sharpest object he came into contact with. It was a scalpel, which wasn't perfect, but it was more useful than the arterial tubes or forceps that were available. During their conversation he'd managed to spot another string of corridors behind the woman, that's where he'd go. He gripped the scalpel tightly in his right hand, and waited.

'There can't be enough to go around, surely' said Stephen.

'Ah, y'see, that is what's great about you lot. You go out in the world, you have sex, you have babies, and… Well, how many children *do* you see around here?' she responded.

'Miscarriages have been higher than ever' said Stephen, shivering at what she was implying.

'If it helps you sleep at night, yes, they have been' she replied, with a wink.

'I. am. Leaving' demanded Stephen, with anger and a sprinkle of fear. He was still in the dark, he still had an advantage.

'I'm afraid you can't be allowed to do that, sir' she replied.

'You are not going to stop me!' he shouted.

Stephen didn't immediately realise his mistake. His mind so overwhelmed by fear, by confusion, by disgust, he didn't quite pay attention to one very important piece of information--As the footsteps behind him got closer, he realised one important word- - "We".

'Yes, I think *we* are' she replied, and threw one of the switches next to her.

The area Stephen stood in lit up just as the man behind him reached out with his hand. Stephen felt the cold fingers on his shoulder, and reacted without thinking. He swung round with his scalpel, blood went spraying over Stephen as the man's throat was sliced in an instant. He fell to his knees, a smile still visible on his face.

'Miles?' said Stephen, his mouth falling open at the site of his best friend.

Miles clutched his throat for only a moment, the blood gushing through his fingers, before he collapsed onto the floor. Even in death, he was still smiling. Tears started streaming from Stephen's eyes, and he let them.

Meanwhile, the woman grabbed a bone saw from the table and threw the switch again. This time the entire room plunged into darkness. Stephen snapped back to reality and he needed to think fast. The corridor was still an option, he just needed to get past her (wherever she was). He was getting nowhere in the dark, every step was a huge risk, every breath was an even bigger one. That's when he remembered, his phone was charged. *Perfect*, he thought, *it's useful after all.*

He yanked it out of his pocket, and switched on the flashlight feature. The sharp LED light filled the room, the sudden burst of blue light made the woman recoil with her hands over her eyes. Stephen used this short window of time to run around the table and escape into the corridor. He shone the flashlight to the left, dead-end. He shone it to the right, bingo. It revealed a long corridor with doors on both sides, and at the end was a ladder. He ran straight forward, not looking back for a second. The corridor lit up as the lights came on a second time. Stephen had reached the ladder, his phone stuffed firmly into his pocket.

He spun round for just a moment, and saw her standing at the end of the corridor with two men behind her dressed in medical gear, all watching him. Turning back to the ladder, he raced up it, the clatter and squeaking of the old metal not bothering him for a second. When he reached the top, he looked around one final time. She still stood there, not chasing him, instead she signalled to the others, smiled and walked away. Stephen looked straight up and saw a square metal hatch. He pushed it with all his might and it slid away.

As he grabbed hold of the ground and pulled himself up, he shoved the hatch back into its slot. It snapped back in with a crash. He rose to his feet and looked around. This was the park alright. The air was cold and bitter, but the sky was clear and pleasant. He stumbled over to the path where he was greeted by a random woman and her dog.

'Morning!' she said, spritely.

Stephen glanced at her, and then her dog. It wasn't the same dog from earlier, this one was a tiny Jack Russell. It's body completely intact, no stitching to be seen. Without thinking he made a run for it, leaping over the fence and sprinting home. His car still sat in the drive as it had done the previous night. Stephen took out his keys and fumbled with them momentarily, before hitting one of the buttons. The car clicked and flashed, the door unlocked. He was soon inside with the doors locked, checking the backseat to make sure. As he saw his own distorted reflection in the windscreen, he breathed out, and put his foot down.

***

'Hello, Stevey!' said Mrs Harris, as she hugged him intently.

'Hi, Mum' he replied, returning it.

'You don't look so good, and what's all this on your shirt? Have you been bleeding?'

'Only a little' said Stephen, he didn't have the heart to tell her it was Miles' blood.

'Well I have some clean shirts lying around, let me go and get you one.'

Stephen's mother headed upstairs, while he went into the kitchen. He ran his hands under the cold tap and washed his face. It felt good to clean himself of all the sweat and blood, it was refreshing. He dried his face and hands with a little tea towel and wandered into the living room. His dad's chair had long since gone, now there was just a gap in the furniture where it used to be, just as there was a gap in their lives.

'Here we are!' said Mrs Harris, pleased that her son had come to visit. 'Get that horrible thing off and try this.'

Stephen struggled to pull of the shirt as it'd stuck to his body, but he managed it and threw it to the floor. His mother handed him the clean one, which he put on doubtfully.

'I can't say I entirely approve, Stephen' she said.

'Of what?' he asked, still pulling the shirt over his head. 'Your new tattoo, it's a bit grim isn't it?'

With the fresh shirt on his body, Stephen stood opposite his mother. His mouth curving up at the sides, as he looked upon her with a great big smile…

The End

CASE #11205

THE NEEDLE'S EYE
BY THOMAS STAPLES

Thomas Staples is a computing student from Norfolk, who uses their spare time to read, and when not doing that, to write. Since discovering a love for the craft many years ago, they have been writing ever since. With a large amount of interest in the horror genre, and a great deal of influence from a variety of authors, Thomas has a unique, yet familiar definitive style of his own. Having never published a piece of work until now, Thomas hopes to further advance his writing skill over time, entertaining as many readers as possible along the way.

Thomas writes short stories with the main theme of psychological horror in mind, as well as making sure the characters don't completely lose their sense of humour, regardless of the situation. He is also soon to begin work on his first novel, (when he isn't distracted, that is) and is looking forward to embracing the five digit word count, rather than running from it.

Thomas also has a minor social media presence, which he uses on a regular basis.

Twitter: https://twitter.com/TheCptAnthony

Tumblr: http://irrelevantnerdinessandsuch.tumblr.com/

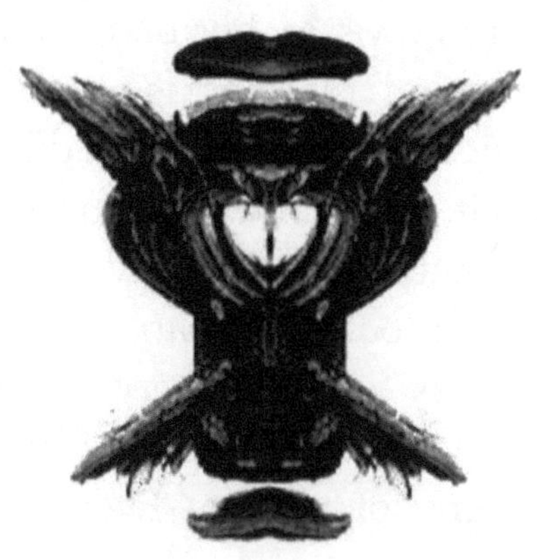

The Hunger by Kristina R. Mosley

WENDY WAS BARELY OUT OF CHILDHOOD when the hunger began. She had always been skinny. Her classmates poked fun at her knobby knees and sharp elbows. Not long after she turned eighteen, however, her body changed. Her stomach felt empty all of the time, cramping as if she hadn't eaten in days. Every precious ounce of extra fat she had begun to melt away, taking muscle with it. Her blonde hair turned brittle and fell out in clumps. Her ribs and hips protruded. Her skin was loose and graying. She no longer looked human.

She went to doctors, who ran every test imaginable. She had no parasites. Her thyroid was fine. Her heart rate was steady. There were no signs of cancer. Everything in her system appeared normal.

"This can't be normal," she cried. "I'm hungry all of the time, and I look like a freak."

No one had any answers for her.

The hunger kept her up at night. She ate all of the food in the cabinets. Her mother would look at her sadly, not saying a word as she went to the grocery store to restock. Wendy sat on the floor and cried.

The burning in her gut wouldn't go away. There was no food, so she ate ice cubes, hoping that would extinguish the fire. They didn't help. Then, she began to eat anything that wouldn't kill her or hurt on the way down. She nibbled at blankets and drank dish soap. Her belly swelled while she ate, but the hunger remained.

Her mother came home half an hour later. She saw the state of her house—empty bottles in the floor, holes in the upholstery— and dropped her bags in shock.

"What's wrong with you?" she shrieked.

Tears glistened in Wendy's eyes. "I wish I knew," she cried. She pushed past her mother and fled from the house, into the nearby woods.

"Wendy!" her mother called into the night.

The girl ran through the forest, twigs snapping under her bare feet and tree limbs slapping her in the face. *Where am I going?* she wondered. *What am I even doing, being alive? I should just throw myself in the lake and stop delaying the inevitable.*

She came across a cabin. It looked inviting with warm light and wonderful aromas emanating from it. She stumbled onto the porch and knocked on the door. A few moments later, a portly old man greeted her.

"My goodness," he said. "You're nothing but skin and bones. Come in and eat something. I was just about to sit down to dinner." "I can't," she whispered, but pain stabbed her in the stomach, and saliva ran down her chin. Everything smelled so good.

"You can," the man replied. "I have plenty, and it looks like you need it worse than I do anyway."

She walked into the cabin.

"My name is Lyle. What's yours?"

"Wendy," she said. She looked around at the cabin's wood paneled walls and shiny oak floors. There was a comfortable-looking couch, and a simple, rustic dining room table with four chairs.

"Do you live here by yourself?" she asked.

Lyle nodded. "My wife passed away a year ago, and our children live in the city."

"Oh, I'm sorry."

"It's fine." He set a plate on the table. "Now, please, sit down and eat."

Wendy did as she was told and pulled out a chair. As she sat, she looked to the plate of food. On it sat a big steak, a huge pile of buttery mashed potatoes, and steamed broccoli. An identical plate was in front of Lyle.

"If you live by yourself, why do you cook so much?" she asked.

The man laughed. "I'm a bit lazy. I cook for multiple days at a time."

"Oh."

"Now, eat," he said. His tone was both stern and kind.

She cut into her steak. It was rare, unlike the medium well she usually ate. She shrugged and took a bite anyway. It was good. She sliced off another piece and ran it through her mashed potatoes, leaving a reddish-brown trail of bloody juice. After she ate the piece of meat and potato, she concentrated on the broccoli, piercing florets with her fork and shoving the buttery little trees into her mouth. Soon, half of her food had disappeared into her still-churning belly.

"You mustn't eat so fast," Lyle said. "It isn't good for you." She slowed down but finished her dinner before he did. Her stomach cramped.

"Oh my, you were hungry, weren't you? Would you like some dessert?"

Wendy nodded.

Lyle stood and picked a chocolate cake off the counter. He set it on the dining table. The brown icing had been lifted in peaks on top. He sliced into the cake, but his left thumb was in the way. He nicked the tip of it, and blood welled to the surface. He hissed and stuck the thumb in his mouth. "Ow," he muttered.

The faintest smell of blood reached her nose. Her stomach growled loudly.

The man chuckled. "Let me clean up my hand, and I'll get some cake for you." He walked to the bathroom.

Wendy looked at the blood on the knife. Why did her stomach growl so much when she smelled it? Why was it growling so much now? She reached out and stuck a bony finger in the blood. It was still warm from Lyle. She put the finger in her mouth. The metallic tang eased the pain in her stomach slightly.

If just a drop of blood makes you feel a little better, how would more make you feel? a voice in her head asked. It sounded like hers, but deeper, gravelly.

Wendy shook her head. *No. I can't be a monster.* She took a deep breath and waited for Lyle to come back.

A few moments later, he re-entered the room, pressing a bandage to his finger. "Now," he said with a smile, "let's try this again." He got another knife from a drawer and bent over the cake.

She looked to his neck, moving slightly with his pulse.

Do it, Wendy. You'll feel better, the voice told her.

She picked up the soiled knife, stood, and stabbed Lyle in the gut. He yelled out as she leapt across the table and bit into his neck, his soft flesh yielding to her sharp teeth. Hot blood sprayed all over her. He tried to push her off, but he had lost too much blood from his injuries. He fell, knocking over chairs and sending dishes and the cake crashing to the floor.

Wendy's stomach felt better as Lyle's blood rushed into it. Soon, though, the blood no longer flowed, and she still felt a little peckish. She picked some flesh out of her teeth and swallowed the tiny bits. The hunger subsided even more.

The meat is what I need, she realized. *But I can't do it, can I?* She took the knife from his abdomen and cut off a piece of his arm, careful to shave off any hair. She popped the flesh into her mouth.

It seemed to melt, reminding her of warm, raw pork. When she swallowed, the burning in her stomach cooled, like dropping an ice cube into a bowl of hot soup.

Wendy tore into Lyle, shoving pieces of him into her mouth. At first, she used the knife to cut off bite-size chunks, but she decided that took too much time. She ripped him open, exposing his organs. Something dark red caught her eye. *His liver,* she thought as she pulled it out. She took a bite. It tasted like the beef liver her mother fed her as a child: strong, metallic. It was fattier, though.

As time passed, she had eaten as much of Lyle as was easily accessible. She felt like she needed something else. *The bone marrow,* she thought. *There's probably more nutrition there.* How would she get to it? Her eyes drifted to the counter. The meat-tenderizing mallet still sat there, the blood and flesh of the steak in its teeth. *That might work.*

After she got the mallet, she went back to the body. She knelt over an exposed thighbone and slammed the mallet into it. It cracked open after a few blows, revealing the red and yellow matter. She scooped out some with a skeletal pinkie and stuck it in her mouth. It tasted fatty, but it was also rich and creamy. Her eyes rolled back in pleasure. She dug into the stuff, shoveling it into her mouth as quickly as she could.

Soon, there was a tightness in her abdomen that she almost didn't recognize. *Am I full?* she wondered. There was no fire, no feeling as if her stomach was going to cave in on itself. *I think I am.* She had no pain or discomfort. Drowsiness washed over her. Content for the first time in months, she fell asleep next to what was left of Lyle.

***

Wendy woke on the floor. Sunlight streamed through the cabin's windows. She turned over and found herself eye-to-eye with the remnants of Lyle's face. His green eyes stayed in their sockets, but most of the skull showed through. She screamed and tried to push away, but a mixture of blood and cake kept her stuck. After prying herself from the floor, she ran to the bathroom.

Her stomach churned. She threw open the toilet lid and stuck her head over the water. Nothing came up. She felt like her brain was going to vomit, even if her body didn't.

She looked in the mirror. Blood covered her, clumped her hair. It coated her rail-thin body. She even managed to get it on her dirty bare feet. Her gut turned again, and she shot back to the toilet. She heaved, but nothing came up.

"Oh God, what am I?" she muttered to her distorted reflection in the water.

After leaning over the toilet for a few minutes, Wendy stood up. Bloody handprints remained where she had gripped the seat. She looked down at her grimy, crusted fingernails. *I have to get clean*, she thought. Still wearing her clothes, she stepped into the shower and turned on the faucet. She let the water get as hot as she could stand it, then she stepped into the shower's stream.

The water washed away the blood, but it didn't wash away her memories. She wondered how she could do that to an old man who was nice enough to let her into his home, to share his food with her. She was an animal. Wendy sobbed for Lyle and for herself, her tears mingling with the bloody water washing down the drain.

After a while, the water turned from red to pink to clear. There was no more blood. "I should get out," she muttered. "I'm getting pruny."

She turned off the water and stepped out of the shower, letting herself drip onto the bathmat. Her eyes kept darting back to the bloody handprints on the toilet seat. She wetted some toilet paper in the sink and scrubbed it off, flushing away the evidence.

Mom's probably worried sick about me, she thought. *I should go home.* Wendy left the bathroom. The low droning of flies greeted her, and then the pungent smell of death hit her nose. "Oh God," she blurted, bile and bits of flesh rising in her throat. She didn't realize there had been enough of Lyle left to cause such an odor. *I have to get out of here*, she thought.

As she rushed from the cabin, a long butane lighter by the fireplace caught her eye. *That would keep anyone from finding out what happened*, the gravelly voice offered.

I can't do that, she countered. *It might cause a forest fire.*

She lowered her head and left the cabin, hoping for the best. As she walked through the woods, she realized she felt better than she had in months. She was stronger, less light headed. It didn't hurt to walk or breathe. *What does it mean?* she wondered.

Soon, she was back in her neighborhood, outside the small white house in which she lived since she was born. She took a deep breath and turned the doorknob. Her mother was nowhere to be found. *Good*, Wendy thought, *maybe she didn't stay up all night.*

Footsteps echoed off the wooden floor. Her mother rushed into the room, her short brown hair disheveled, her blue eyes rimmed in red. "Wendy," she huffed.

"Hi, Mom."

"Where were you?" her mother asked, hugging her.

"Out," was all Wendy said.

"All night? Where did you sleep?" "In the woods."

Her mother pulled away. "Why are you wet?"

Wendy didn't respond for a few moments. "I thought taking a swim in the lake would make me feel better."

"Did it help?"

"Yes, it did."

"Well, you should take a shower to get that dirty water off you. Who knows what might be on your skin."

Even though she wasn't really dirty, Wendy didn't fight her mother. She merely nodded and walked into the bathroom. After closing the bathroom door behind her, she pried off her wet dress and turned on the shower. She washed the dirt off her feet, but then she sat on the closed toilet seat, letting the steam fill up the bathroom.

Images of Lyle's desecrated body flashed through her head, no matter how much she tried to keep them away. The metallic taste

of blood still filled her mouth. She shuddered. The view of her shoulders in her peripheral vision caught her attention. The bones didn't seem to stick out as much. She looked down. Her belly was still concave, but it pooched out a bit more. Her hipbones were less prominent.

It can't be, she thought.

∗∗∗

As the days progressed, Wendy became closer to her old self. Bald spots on her scalp began to fill in. Her cheeks weren't as sunken. She wasn't back to one hundred percent, but she felt stronger.

For a few weeks after Lyle, the only hunger Wendy felt was the normal, everyday kind. Then, it became more intense. The burning in her stomach returned. Like before, she ate all of the food in the house to no avail. What little weight she had gained was lost again.

Lyle, she thought. *Lyle is what made me better.*

One day, her mother was in the kitchen as she went to the refrigerator for the fifth time in a row.

"You're hungry, aren't you?" the woman asked. She got out of her chair and walked across the room.

"Of course I am." Wendy slammed the refrigerator door, rattling the magnets. "I don't even know why I bother looking. Food won't do anything."

"Oh, sweetie," her mother said. "I thought you were getting better."

"I thought so, too," Wendy replied, tears blurring her vision. She felt her mother's arms wrap around her.

"It'll be all right," the older woman whispered. "You'll be strong again."

Her mother didn't understand, could never understand. Wendy didn't cry because of her relapse, but for what she knew she'd have to do to overcome it.

***

"There has to be another way," she said aloud.

You saw what happened after Lyle. It's the only option, the gravelly voice countered.

Maybe it doesn't have to be another person, she thought. She noticed a strip of cuticle hanging beside her fingernail. It only took a bit of Lyle to make her feel better. Surely she wouldn't

70

need much. She bit down on the piece of skin and pulled, going into the quick. She hissed and tugged, bringing the flesh into her mouth and swallowing. Nothing changed.

Blood welled where the flesh had been torn away. *Maybe that's what I need.* She stuck her finger in her mouth. The metallic tang hit her tongue. She swallowed. When it had been Lyle's, that small amount had helped, but her own did nothing.

She realized it had to be another person's. "No, no, no!" she cried. "I can't do it. I can't be that thing."

What other choice do you have? the gravelly voice asked. *You've eaten cows and chickens before.*

But these are people, she argued.

They're made of meat and bones just like the other animals.

The idea hurt her, but she knew she had to do it. She needed to live, and being a walking skeleton wasn't a life. That night, she took a large butcher's knife from a block in the kitchen. Then, she snuck out of her bedroom window while her mother was asleep. The night was warm and muggy, and she began sweating before she left her neighborhood. *Could be nerves, too,* she told herself.

Soon, Wendy found herself in the center of town. The town square was eerie at night. Streets that normally bustled with people were quiet and deserted. *Why did I come here?* Wendy wondered.

Then, she heard keys jangle. She ducked behind a bush. A man locked the door of a jewelry store. She tried to get a closer look at him. He was middle-aged with glasses, short, and somewhere between pudgy and athletic-build, like he used to be more active in his younger days.

He might work, she thought.

She crept up to the man. His back was still to her. She stabbed him with the butcher knife, trying to hit his lung. *If he can't breathe, he can't scream*, the gravelly voice told her.

The man turned, his brown eyes wide in fear. He tried to call out, but only gurgles emerged from his throat. After a few more thrusts of the knife, he was on the ground.

Wendy slipped the knife into her back pocket and dragged the body into a nearby alley. She took her time with him. When she was finished, she stashed his remains behind some trashcans and walked out of the alley.

She walked home in the shadows, hoping no one would see her. After she crawled back into her bedroom, she cleaned both herself and the knife and went to bed.

The next morning, she woke up feeling refreshed and energized.

Her stomach sank. She was glad she felt better, but she hated why.

She didn't want another person to die so she could live.

But it must be done, the gravelly voice told her.

"So it does."

***

And so it did. Every time the hunger returned, she would go out into the night and find some stranger. It was easier when she didn't know their names. Wendy resigned herself to the fact that she needed to eat human flesh to live. She soon figured out who was suitable for eating and who wasn't. She tended to stay away from the very old. They were tough and chewy, and they often took medications that made them taste strange. She avoided anyone who looked like a drug addict for similar reasons. She also left children alone. *I already eat people,* she thought. *I don't want to be a complete monster.*

She tried to kill them as mercifully as possible. They didn't need to suffer for her.

The hunger came back at an increasing rate. First, it was weeks between feedings, then weekly, then every few days. She was afraid she'd soon have to feed daily. *Will I actually have to go out and get someone every day?* she wondered. *What about when I start college in the fall? Normal kids have enough trouble balancing school and personal lives, and their personal lives don't involve killing and eating people. I have to find a way to stop,* she told herself.

How, though? Things would be different if the human flesh didn't help her, but it did. A slight rosiness graced her cheeks. Meat returned to her bones. She went back to her pre-hunger weight. She didn't want to waste away again.

***

Wendy felt and looked much better, but guilt followed her everywhere. She lived in a small town, so word had gotten around quickly. Everyone spoke in hushed whispers about what was happening.

One day, the girl was in the grocery store, picking up a few items. She overheard two women speaking in the produce section.

"This is some scary business, Ethel. People being *eaten,*" one of them said, whispering the last word.

"Oh, I know, Myrtle," replied the other. "It can't be an animal killing everyone. Surely, it's a monster."

"Of course it isn't a monster," Myrtle said. "It's a person. The police found knife marks and fingerprints." *Fingerprints?* Wendy wondered.

"How did you know that?" Ethel asked. "That wasn't in the newspaper."

"My grandson works for the sheriff's department, remember?" The girl had last eaten someone the day before. She was in a hurry, and in her haste, she hadn't covered her tracks as carefully as she normally did. The police would find her. Everyone would know what kind of thing she had become. She tried to leave the store as nonchalantly as possible.

"Hello, Wendy," one of the women called out.

She turned around to realize that Myrtle was a friend of her late grandmother. "Oh, hi," she said.

Myrtle shuffled over to Wendy. "You look so much better! Did you ever find out what was wrong?"

The girl shrugged. "I guess I was eating something that wasn't agreeing with me."

"Oh."

Wendy's heart raced. *They can tell.* "I'd love to stay and chat, but I must be going." She rushed away from the woman, plowing straight into a display of watermelons. The fruit crashed to the floor and busted.

Produce workers descended on the sticky scene. "I'm so sorry," Wendy stammered, trying to help clean the mess. She picked up a damaged melon and handed it to a pimply-faced teen with a wispy mustache. Something red was on her hand. *Must be watermelon.* She looked down. It was blood. *No, that was yesterday. I cleaned up.* She rubbed the back of her hand on her jeans, but the spot was stubborn. *I can't let them see. They'll know.*

She abandoned her basket and ran crying from the store. "I'm sorry!" she called.

*****

Wendy burst into her bedroom, slammed the door, and threw herself onto her bed. *I can't do this anymore,* she thought. *I can't be this* thing *anymore.* She had started to eat people in order to live, but this was no life. If she were gone, she couldn't hurt anyone else. She would just stop eating. Normal food wouldn't help her anyway. The world would be better off without her.

The hunger returned, just as it always did. She kept herself locked in her room, trying to avoid temptation. It consumed her very being. It was all she could think about. She couldn't sleep due to the pain in her gut.

She drank gallons of cold water and ate pounds of ice, trying to extinguish the fire, but she should have known they wouldn't work.

As the weeks passed, Wendy became thinner and thinner. There was nothing between flesh and bone. Her eyes bulged. The hunger drained the life from her, but it wouldn't let her die.

"Why aren't you eating anything?" her mother asked. "Surely you're hungry."

You have no idea, Wendy thought, but she remained silent.

One day, the girl stared into space, the hunger filling her thoughts. Her mother entered her line of vision.

What are you waiting for? the gravelly voice asked. *She's right there. Get her.*

"I can't. She's my mother."

"What was that, Wendy?" her mother asked.

The girl's eyes went wide. *Did I say that out loud?* Her pain confused her. "Nothing," she muttered.

C'mon, you know you want to. She might be a bit tough, but the fat she probably has marbled through her muscle would make her taste good.

Wendy's stomach twisted. She felt sick, but she was still so hungry. "Stop it."

"Honey, you need to speak up. I can't hear you."

Imagine how her marrow would taste. You know that's always your favorite part.

"Shut up."

Do it, Wendy. Do it do it do it do it do it do it.

Her breath quickened, and her heart raced. She was close to hyperventilating now. The girl gripped her mother's arm, her sharp, bony fingers pressing into the flesh.

"Wendy, what's wrong with you?" her mother asked, eyes wide in fear.

The girl growled and leapt, biting her mother on the arm.

The woman screamed.

She's making too much noise, the gravelly voice said. *Do something about it.*

She found her mouth on her mother's throat, clamping down on the windpipe. It popped, and her mother stopped screaming. Wendy huddled over the body, not bothering to go to the kitchen and get a knife. She tore into her mother's flesh with her teeth and hands. It was still hot. It was a little chewy, but it tasted fantastic.

She had shoved about a fourth of her mother down her throat when someone knocked on the door.

"Police. A neighbor reported screams coming from the residence," a man said.

"Everyone's okay," she called. Bits of flesh and blood sprayed from her mouth.

"Could you come to the door? We'd like to make sure everything's all right."

Wendy panicked. There was no way she could hide the body and get cleaned up. "No one's home," she yelled.

Really? the gravelly voice wondered.

"We're coming in," another police officer, a woman, said.

Wendy looked around frantically like she was trying to find a hole to crawl into.

The door flew open. The two police officers stood before her with guns drawn. Then, they saw what was happening, Wendy above her mother, flesh and blood all over her face. The male looked like he was trying to keep his lunch down, while the woman looked at her with disgust.

"Oh my God," the woman whispered. "Why did you do it?" Hot tears ran down Wendy's face. "I was hungry."

The End.

CASE #30069

THE HUNGER

BY KRISTINA R. MOSLEY

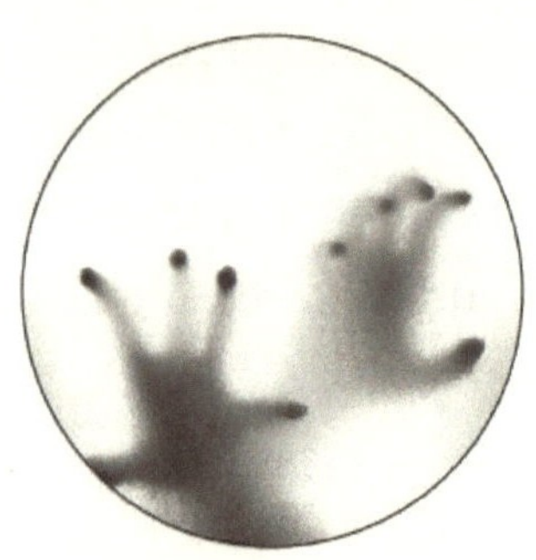

Kristina R. Mosley lives in Kensett, Arkansas, a tiny place no one has heard of. Her work has been featured in numerous publications, including Weirdyear, The WiFiles, Bloodbond, Strangely Funny 2 1/2, and Jitter. Her novelette Strange Days is available on Amazon. She is active on Twitter at twitter.com/elstupacabra.

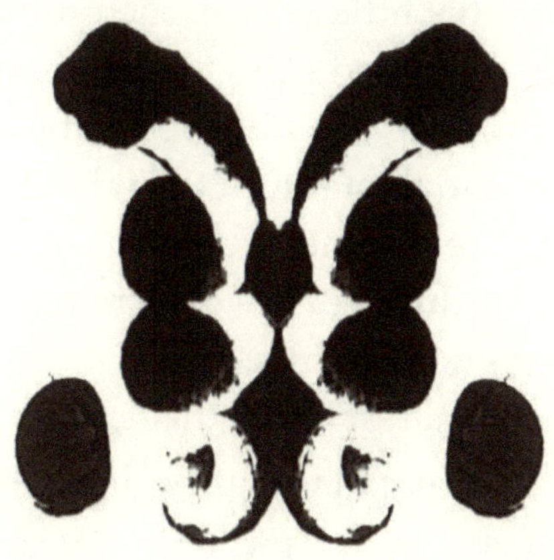

An Egg Of Stone And Steel by Stephen Williams

PRINCE ART HAD BEEN EXPLORING HIS FAMILY'S PALACE ever since his little legs learned to navigate staircases. From the canopies of stained glass to the oceans of marble, there was always something new to discover in the castle. He'd toddle from spire to spire, and then return to his bedroom to scribble his progress on one of the original blueprints tacked to the wall. At the age of eight, two thirds of the plan remained uncharted. He had quite the quest ahead of him.

One destination that sparked his interest was a spacious courtyard deep in the palace guts. But after following the twisting hallways, he found the only entrance sealed with a dozen rusted locks. Standing on his tiptoes and squinting through the door's peephole, he was able to make out a small castle surrounded by dead grass. What a funny place, he thought. He'd have to talk to his mother about it.

That night, after he'd brushed his teeth and crawled into bed, he asked the Queen about the mysterious ruin.

"I suppose you could use a bedtime story," she sighed. "But it is a bit scary. Do you think you can handle it?"

Prince Art was always up for a challenge. Besides, the scary ones were his favorites. The boy cocooned himself in blankets and the Queen began.

"Not that long ago, there was a king," she said. "He was kind and loved throughout the land—but this love had also made him naïve and prideful. Despite all of its pleasures, love can wear away a person's strength the way a river smooths stones. The king that ruled the neighboring empire was strong, and he took note of the Kind King's laziness. He decided to invade, and in almost no time at all, his army stood waiting at his enemy's portcullis.

"But the Strong King was not without mercy, and he made the Kind King a fair offer. All he had to do was surrender and he'd be allowed to take his family to live out the rest of their days in the country. The Kind King sneered at the proposition.

"'You'll never breach these walls!' the Kind King cried from the battlements. 'And if you want me to give up my kingdom, you'll have to come in and get us.'

"The Strong King had the numbers, the weapons, the will—but he knew a prolonged siege would be a bloody endeavor that could decay his troops' morale. That's when he came up with a brilliant plan. Instead of breaching the walls and dragging the stubborn royal family, guards, and servants out into the sunlight, he'd entomb them in their own beds. Immediately, The Strong King's builders began to construct the largest palace the world had ever seen—one that would devour the tiny castle on the hill. All estates need a name, and as the materials were shipped in, the Strong King decided to call his new home Tartarus.

"As hundreds of stonemasons cut the granite that would form the innermost walls, the Kind King called every soul in his palace to the throne room for an announcement.

"'Let them build,' he growled as his friends and family looked on silently. 'We have drink, we have food, we have sunshine, and we have each other. We'll make it through this darkness.'

"Before construction could begin, they needed a foundation. The Strong King's men fitted every wrist for a thousand miles with shackles and forced picks and shovels into their hands. The army of slaves cleaved the earth until they reached the edge of Hell. Then, they filled the trenches with obsidian and molten iron. This base dammed up all the natural water flowing into the tiny palace and severed its pipes like a guillotine through veins.

"No matter," the Kind King chuckled. 'Who needs water when you have wine? Let's celebrate!'

"They danced and partied until the cellar was empty. Wine dribbled down their chins and stained the thick, feathery carpet.

They sunk up to their shins in the plush material, and running their toes through it felt like heaven. They still had sunshine, food, and companionship. The Kind King could hear his children playing. Everything was going to be okay.

"As the Strong King positioned pillars as tall as mountains, the Kind King's family passed the time on their veranda. They soaked up the sun, chatted, played cards—until the builders sealed the sky with a black dome. The royal family's estate had been transformed into an egg of stone and steel. The claustrophobia was suffocating.

"'Enough of this gloom,' the Kind King declared. 'Light some candles, let's have a feast!'

"Every room was filled with wax sticks and fire—every room smothered in glowing hope. Roasted pigs, berry preserves, and fresh bread poured out of the kitchen. They ate until there was nothing left and the buttons popped from their clothes, ricocheting throughout the dining room. With his belly full, the Kind King could still hear his children playing. Everything was going to be okay.

"It was what came next that the King wasn't prepared for—silence. No more demands, no more construction. They were left alone in their little castle and the outside world was moving on without them. The memory of their dynasty faded like the chirping birds after the dome had been riveted into place. Melancholy rained down. Their supplies dwindled. Time became their true enemy.

"As the Kind King's stomach growled and his tongue grew dusty, his staff vanished one by one. In the shadows, he could see the silhouettes of his remaining servants licking greasy fingers. They clutched wine glasses in their talons, making the red liquid inside waltz along the walls.

"'I thought we were out of food and wine?' he called weakly from his throne.

"'We are,' the servants replied.

"He couldn't hear his children playing.

"One by one, the candles began to wink out. With them all burned to worthless stubs, the Kind King limped from his throne. He called for help, but only the echo of his own withered voice replied. Where had everyone gone? Had they found a way out and surrendered? He needed someone. His hunger and loneliness were threatening to peel his mind like an onion.

"It only took one step on the stained carpet to find his companions. He felt a crunch beneath his loafer, and then another. Buried in the fabric were dozens of brittle skulls. The smooth surface of many of them had been riddled with chew marks. His palace had become a graveyard.

"The Kind King could no longer stand the weight of his crown. He collapsed to the floor, took a final breath, and turned to dust. His pride and love had been enough to sustain him for a while, but in the end, his bones joined the others."

The Queen finished with a smile. The Prince had buried himself in pillows, shivering as the tale reached its conclusion. "Could something like that ever happen to us?" he whispered.

"Of course not, you silly boy," his mother said. "But make sure you go straight to sleep, otherwise you may not grow up to be one of the strong kings."

She gave him a wink and a sloppy kiss on the forehead. As he drifted to sleep, the Queen turned to the window to watch the sunset in peace. She was able to make out the base of a new wall along the horizon, a dark smooth line. It reminded her of the way blood pooled between tiles. Her husband, the Strong King, had also been blinded by his own conquests—and their neighbor, the Bloodthirsty King, had noticed. Now that he'd borrowed their tactics, the sun would be setting a few hours earlier by the end of the year. Before her precious prince had learned to shave, the sun would be gone.

The End.

CASE #49664

AN EGG OF STONE AND STEEL
BY STEPHEN WILLIAMS

Stephen Williams is a janitor in a small desert town where the only thing to do for fun is catch rattlesnakes. He holds a degree in creative writing from the University of California, Riverside where he won the Chancellor's Performance Award for excellence in fiction. His work has appeared in numerous publications, including Menacing Hedge, Sanitarium, Underneath the Juniper Tree, and Goreyesque. Currently, he serves as an editor for Rind Literary Magazine. His debut novel, Among the Ruins, will be released in 2015 by Villipede Publications.

Extreme Horror: The Essential Ten by Alex Davis

Of all the subgenres of horror, for me the most underexposed and underrated is the more extreme end of the market. Extreme horror movies are often produced independently, produced on relatively low budgets and designed to truly push boundaries and explore taboos in a way that most media – and certainly film in the mainstream – is afraid to.

In my year of reviewing at Film Gutter, I've had the dubious pleasure of watching some of the most disturbing and edgiest features released in extreme horror. It's been a genuine eye-opener – some movies here I had seen previously, but I've been lucky enough to stumble across some stunning features over the last twelve months. And although I consider myself someone who's pretty thick-skinned, there have also been occasions where I've been genuinely shocked, horrified and disgusted.

So, if you're a fan of horror in all its forms and are wondering where to start with extreme horror, the following ten are ideal viewing for those of you willing to test your stomach and constitution by exploring this fascinating subgenre. **Don't say I haven't warned you – these movies are not for the faint of heart!**

The list is presented purely alphabetically rather than in any order of preference.

1) **A Serbian Film (Serbia, 2010).** What better place to begin that one of the most controversial films of recent years? Srdjan Spasojevic's debut feature marked him as a director to watch, and the deeply uncomfortable message this one sends about human sexuality is bound make an impact on the viewer. There's far more to this movie than the infamous (and practically throaway) baby scene. Visceral, violent and vivid, A Serbian Film is an unmitigated trip into depraved nightmare that takes in murder, incest, rape and much more besides.

2) **Flowers (USA, 2015).** Possibly the least-known film on this list, but not for long. Phil Stevens' first feature hit in 2015 and presented the tale of six lost souls with such a dark and

demented poetry – and not a line of dialogue in sight – that I was riveted to the screen the whole time. Flowers is the perfect example of a movie without words and shows what can be done with a look, a move and a reaction. Visually fascinating and enigmatic, with a conclusion bound to leave you wondering for a long time, this movie is extreme horror at its most artistic and most hauntingly beautiful. Not long released from Unearthed Films, and well worth the investment of time and money.

"FLOWERS was written, designed and structured in every aspect to be whatever the viewer wanted it to be or saw what they wanted it to be or believe it to be. It's a horror film. It's a nightmare. It's a journey. It's an experiment in filmmaking." Director Phil Stevens on Flowers.

3) **Martyrs (France, 2008).** The gold standard of extreme horror from a country with a mean reputation in the field, Martyrs is phenomenal filmmaking and – for me – is one of the best films made in recent times full stop. Martyrs has the foot on the gas from the very get go and barely lets up, and takes in one of the most difficult to watch finales in movie history. The philosophical and religious points behind the horror

add a whole other level to the terrible proceedings. A harrowing tale of torment and insanity, it'll have you watching through your fingers in places but you will not be able to stop watching.

4) **Megan is Missing (USA, 2011).** You want bleak? Then this is surely the movie for you. This story of a young girl falling foul of an internet predator does well to develop characters and believability in its early stages, playing out for the most part as a sort of 21st-century mystery story with a distinctly topical theme. However, this movie closes with what is surely the most gut-wrenching, soul-crushing twenty minutes of unflinching cinema you'll ever see. You might well need a hug after the credits roll on this one. Definitely not on a par with some of the other suggestions for gore and violence, but plenty brutal enough in its own way.

5) **Melancholie Der Engel (Germany, 2009).** The magnum opus of extreme horror legend Marian Dora, this is a simple tale of a man trying to enjoy himself and find some meaning before his life comes to a close. Unfortunately that 'enjoyment' is of the most horrifying variety imaginable, taking in rape, abuse, human excrement and animal cruelty. Hugely infamous, you'll find this film at the top or near the top of most 'disturbing film' lists out there. At almost three hours, the movie exhibits a strong artistic vision as well as some of the most nihilistic and disgusting scenes ever committed to celluloid. An absolute experience, but not one for the faint of heart.

6) **Singapore Sling (Greece, 1990).** Hard to know quite what to say on this one. Nikos Nikolaidis' best-known movie is shot like a black and white film noir, was intended to be a comedy by its director and went down in history as an extreme horror classic. The only film by the director to receive a US release, *Singapore Sling* follows a mother and daughter with a twisted BDSM relationship (not to mention the dead, mummified father) and the unfortunate detective who stumbles into their deranged web. This is possibly one of the most unusual and uneasy films you're ever likely to see.

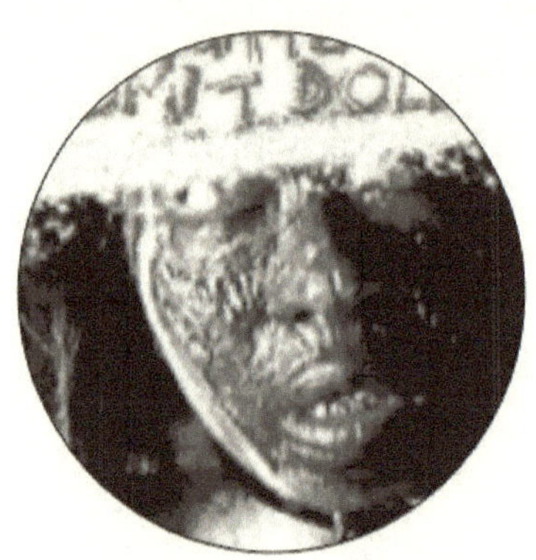

7) **Slaughtered Vomit Dolls (USA, 2006).** Are you feeling brave? *Really* brave? Lucifer Valentine's underground cult movie is the first in the gloriously titled Vomit Gore Trilogy, which couldn't make it any clearer what you're about to embark upon here. Possibly the most sickening film ever made, with grotesque visuals combining with a soundtrack designed to make it as hard to watch as can be – brace yourself for white noise and grating slow motions. Vile, perverted and unapologetic, I don't think there's any experience quite like this one out there - but, with all that

said, there is some intangible quality here that will leave you reeling.

8) **Subconscious Cruelty (Canada, 2000).** A movie that is challenging in both its artistic delivery and its disturbing content, Karim Hussein's masterwork might just be one of the finest experimental horror films ever constructed.

The story of the disturbed relationship between brother and sister, and the hideous 'act' that will change both their lives forever and flip the film on its head. There's a depth of thought and artistry here that is rarely seen in horror – cloying and sinister in it first half, surreal and nightmarish in the second, this is a movie that will definitely stand a second watch to peel back more of its strange layers.

9) **Thanatomorphose (Canada, 2012).** If one movie on this list had me close to hitting the stop button, this was it. As the credits rolled I had my hands over my ears asking out loud 'Is it over?' – and how I wish that was an exagerration. A simply told story of one woman's journey into a hell of decay and insatiable sexual desire, this low-budget Canadian piece packs plenty of shock value for its minimal budget. The lead actress Kayden Rose carries a tremendously difficult role here, and the bodily horror that unravels here is bound to leave an impression. Utterly unflinching in its gore and viscera, this is extreme horror at its most precise and methodical.

"There are two reactions to the film: either people despise it or they like it. I'm really proud of that because that mean we hit something. You don't want to be a crowd pleaser with that kind of film."
Director Eric Falardeau on Thanatomorphose

The Human Centipede 2: Full Sequence (USA, 2011). Whatever you might have heard about this series, all three are well worth checking out in their own way, a trilogy offering up three hugely different movies hanging on the infamous central concept. The most extreme – and the most retch-inducing – is doubtless the second offering, *Full Sequence* – and I say that despite the UK censors making more than 30 cuts. A black and white nightmare to give

David Lynch a bad night's sleep, where *First Sequence* largely left bodily functions to the imagination the follow-up practically revels in gore and human faeces. It's also a clever 'meta' response to the furore surrounding the first movie, but also contains an interesting psychological backstory delivered without a single word from the lead character.

"They watched the first film and said 'Where's the sh*t? We want to see that flying!' And I gave it to them, like heroin addicts, and then they went over the top! This is crazy! They asked for it."
Director Tom Six on The Human Centipede: Full Sequence

All director quotes are taken from the Gutter Talk section of the Ginger Nuts of Horror website, which offers accompanying interviews to the Film Gutter review series (also hosted at GNOH). For more, visit www. gingernutsofhorror.com

Alex Davis has been a horror fan for as long as he can remember, be it books or film. His first bookshelf was loaded with the works of James Herbert and Stephen King, and he's also had a range of horror short fiction published as an author. Having watched many of the films considered the most disturbing ever made, his *Film Gutter* review series is a journey to try and find the very best in extreme horror as well as uncover that one film that he simply can't make it to the end of. Running since the start of 2015, the series has new expanded to include the *Gutter Talk* interview section, which has taken in directors and actors such as Dieter Laser, Bree Olson, Tom Six, Phil Stevens, Jimmy Weber and many more.

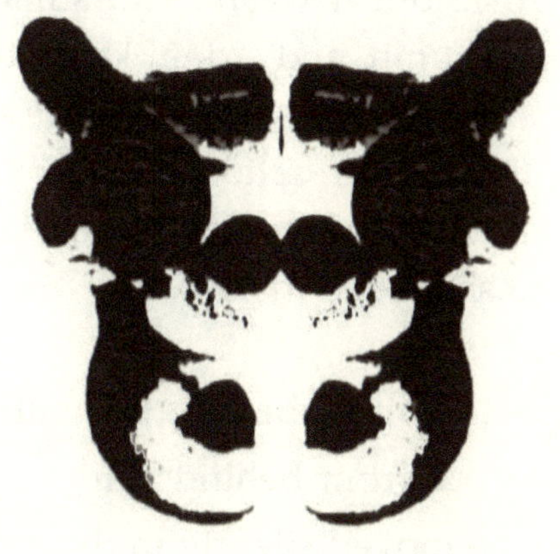

Deer Kingdom by Valerie Alexander

THE CHRISTMAS LIGHTS WERE GOING UP IN TOWN, plastic reindeer heads and snowmen glowing in the gunmetal-blue November dusk. But it wasn't Christmastime yet or even winter. It was still autumn, and Adam knew that by the sodden leaves under his boots and the smoky bonfire smell that lingered over the barren fields after school. And by the dark yellow afternoon light that fell in the woods, so that the oak and ash and beech trees seemed shrouded in mist.

"Hi," Lily said.

She always greeted him when he was still twenty or so feet from her, stepping out from behind a tree and smiling so she didn't scare him. She moved silently in the woods, her bare feet making only the occasional stick crack, and there was the eeriness of her pale face framed in the forest gloom, which she seemed to sense even though there was no mirror out here for her to see how she'd changed. So it was nice of her, Adam thought, to not scare him.

"Hey," he said.

"Are you early or late today?"

"Early," he said. "But it's getting dark out." "Yeah."

She turned and he followed her back to the cluster of trees where she'd put together a lean-to these last few weeks. Two wooden doors comprised the base, with some random planks and a plastic tarp that provided a wall, all of it scavenged from the Barringers' junkyard at the other end of the woods. At the edge Lily had lined up her collected treasures – some magazines he'd brought her, a pile of beechnuts, a crow with a broken neck that wasn't rotting.

Lily was dead, but that didn't bother Adam. What did bother him was that she was famous-dead, and a cold dread clenched his stomach at the thought of being found with her. Of accidentally saying her name at school or around his mother. The county was postered with MISSING signs that featured a photo of her smiling over her hamster's cage along with her eighth grade school picture, *LILITH ABIGAIL BROSSARD, 13 years old. 5'1, 97 lbs, brown hair, brown eyes. Reward for information.* Search teams and dogs had swept the fields, the woods, the highway rest stops and the water reservoir. Her mother and stepfather had appeared on morning news shows, her mother tearfully choking out answers, her stepfather gruff. The school had changed their pick-up and bus stop policies so no student had to walk home alone, though Adam still walked by himself anyhow. He knew there wasn't a killer on the loose. Not one that was looking for other kids to kill, at least.

"I saw five deer today and a fox," Lily said. "Do you think I'll see a bear or do you think they're hibernating already?"

"I don't know."

She scrambled over the lean-to and retrieved a large, dead beetle with an iridescent shell. "An early Christmas present," she said.

"Thanks." He put it in his pocket, knowing he would dispose of it on the way home. His mother had already complained about the smell he brought home with him. A dead bug would be a giveaway that he was going into the woods.

"You should get me a present," Lily said. "Like an iPad. Then I could use it when you're not here."

He didn't know if she was joking. "You can't charge it out here." "You'd recharge it for me and bring it back." She watched him and when he didn't respond, she nudged him. "More magazines would be nice too. But not from your mom." "Where am I supposed to get this stuff?" "The store, stupid."

He changed the subject. "What if someone sees this when they're looking for you? Or deer hunters?" He tapped the doors they were sitting on.

"They'll just think some kids built it." She shrugged. "And that's true."

Lily had been his neighbor when she was alive – her family lived just four houses up and around the corner from his. Sometimes he had seen her walking home with other girls. But she hadn't spoken to him, because she was two grades ahead of him and they didn't know each other.

"They still talk about you in school," Adam said. "We didn't have another assembly, but all the teachers tell us not to walk home by ourselves."

"Some people came through here again with dogs."

"What if they saw you? Where do you go?"

"Underground. I'm part of all this now, just like the animals."

"You're not like an animal."

"Kind of, I am. If I had stayed in my grave, I would have turned into earth and my soul would have gone into the deer and the rabbits."

That was the part Adam didn't understand - how a soul could be absorbed like spilled liquid. He knew why she hadn't stayed in her grave, sort of, because she had explained that some kind of forest man had pulled her out. Though that didn't make much sense to him either.

"Why don't you let them see you?" he asked. "You could say what happened -"

"*He* wouldn't let me, for one," she said. "Besides, they would try to take me out of the woods and I can't do that. I told you, I need the woods to stay like this. Like you need air to breathe."

"You could tell them about your stepfather."

"I don't want to," she said. "One day my stepfather will come back to check on the grave. And I'll be here."

***

The supermarket didn't sell the mp3 players and tablets Lily wanted, but Adam had no way to get to the mall. He bought magazines instead, the kind with celebrities on the cover, with the twenty dollar bill he'd stolen from his mother's purse. Then he went through the aisles one more time, looking for other gifts. He couldn't bring Lily food, because she didn't eat. He thought she would need new clothes eventually, even though she didn't feel the cold, because the jeans and violet top she had been buried in were dirty and stained. But she hadn't mentioned wanting new clothes.

At home he hid the magazines between his mattress and box springs. When he went downstairs for dinner, his mother was still in her nursing scrubs and watching the news.

"I feel so guilty for not doing more," she said as she watched a search group move in formation across a field with cameras, dogs and thermal equipment. "Maybe I'll help with one of the night searches this weekend when I'm not on shift." She opened the oven and took out a glass casserole dish of potatoes and broccoli.

"They're not going to find her."

"They might. They don't always take them far, child abductors." "Why does everyone think she was kidnapped?"

"Her mother saw the car, honey. She heard Lily scream from the front yard and ran outside." She shivered. "I can't imagine what that poor woman is going through. The not knowing."

"Lily Brossard is probably dead by now. They should stop looking."

His mother looked at him in surprise, then put a hand on his matted blond head and pushed him into a chair. "Eat. And remember, don't take the shortcut by the woods. I want you to take the long way home from school - it's only a few minutes longer. You'll do that for me, right?"

***

He had been warned away from the shortcut four times now. The first was the day after Lily went missing, when the Amber Alert wasn't quickly resolved like everyone expected. In school that day they had been told how to stay safe and his aunt had picked him up from school, which embarrassed him even though the middle school curb was two-deep with parents' cars that day. When his mother finally agreed to let him walk home again, he took the shortcut that went by the woods, only to see a pale-faced girl standing just inside the trees, watching him.

It's Lily Brossard. I found her.

He headed across the field to her, because even if they weren't on speaking terms, she should recognize him from living just a few houses away. "Everybody's looking for you," he'd said. "Did you run away?"

"No. My stepfather killed me and buried me out here." She walked deeper into the woods and he had followed.

Lily claimed that she didn't remember anything between her stepfather slamming her head with a brick and then waking up in the earth. She said she was awake underground for a while, earthworms and beetles crawling over her skin. "I could feel him reviving me," she said. "I'd still be dead if it wasn't for him."

Him didn't have a name, but Lily referred to him quite a bit. He was the mysterious forest king who had pulled her out of her grave. He had preserved the dead crow sitting on the lean-to, she said, because he ruled over the animals and the trees and the creek. Or rather, Lily corrected herself, he was the animals and the trees and the creek. It sounded to Adam like a story she'd made up, but he pretended to believe her and asked only why *he* couldn't have stopped her stepfather from killing her. Lily replied that she died in her bedroom.

"It would have been different if it happened out here," she said. "He would have protected me."

He pointed at the crow. "So how come that's still dead?" "Because it would fly away if he revived it, duh. I want it to sit right there."

November went colder and grayer. The treeline was skeletal now, and it was easy to see twenty yards or more into the forest. The search teams had mostly given up on this area and hunters had filled the trees at dawn once deer season opened. But Adam knew from a local news report that search efforts would be renewed in these woods one more time before the first snow fell.

On Thursday he skipped last-period study hall and came to the woods early. Lily asked him again for an iPad.

"I don't know where to get one," he said.

"You have a whole house full of stuff," she said. "You could sell something. It's a big house, your mom has to have something you could sell in there."

"It's not that big."

"Yes, it is. I went and looked at it last night." He felt a creeping unease. "Why?" "Something to do."

Walking out of the woods was always harder than walking in. His back to her. The possibility that her cold hand might land on his shoulder, that she might materialize in front of him or step out from behind a tree up ahead on the path. And right as he approached the treeline, his anxiety ballooned into panic, heart pounding loudly with the fear that she would change her mind about letting him go –

But he wasn't hers to keep or let go. Dead or not, Lily was still just the girl from around the corner, a few inches taller than him, but still just a girl. She had no supernatural powers. If she ever tried to hold him back, what could she do? He'd push her hard and make a run for the field, then his yard. She had no weapons. Maybe he should start carrying a knife to school.

Then he felt bad. Lily was his friend. She'd captured a live rabbit for him to hold, showed him where the wolves traveled at dusk. She'd told him a hilarious story about a high school party in the woods on Halloween night. He'd told her about catching snakes in the creek every summer and she said she wanted to do it with him when it got warm again.

And crossing the field to his backyard, a growing denial spread through him: a conviction that Lily wasn't real. It was impossible for a dead girl to be lingering in the woods, a dead girl who talked and walked around and didn't seem to be rotting, so either he was hallucinating or, more likely, Lily was alive. Her stepfather had buried her alive and she had escaped and now looked pale and weird from the cold. That rank odor was from not showering, the dead animals she arranged in the treehouse. Once it started snowing and she couldn't go barefoot anymore, she would go home.

That was the logical explanation, but just as he reached the yellowed grass of his yard and looked up at his house windows glowing in the dusk, he felt that Lily didn't exist at all. She just couldn't.

He looked closely at the path that cut through the field. Between the puddles from a recent storm, the imprints of his sneakers were clear in the mud. Next to them, occasionally obliterated by them, he could see another set of tracks: small bare footprints that stopped at the edge of the yard.

So she really had come and looked at his house. She wasn't strictly limited to the woods; she could come through the field too.

His mother emerged from the garage with a bulging black trash bag in her arms. She frowned. "Why are you standing by the field?

You didn't take the shortcut, did you?" She sniffed. "What is that smell - a skunk?"

"I guess," he said right before he realized his error.

"You did go by the woods! Goddamit, Adam! Why don't you realize how serious this is?"

"I was hungry," he said. "I wanted to get home fast."

She dropped the garbage bag on the grass and gripped him by the back of the neck. He was startled to see tears in her eyes. "Adam, the search dogs picked up that little girl's scent in those woods. You can't take the shortcut. For god's sake, people like that - they don't just take girls."

To his horrified embarrassment, she burst into sobs. She turned away, pushing her messy brown hair out of her eyes and sniffling angrily.

"Mom, I'm sorry," he said. "I won't go that way again."

***

That week he faked feeling sick in gym class. In the locker room he looked feverishly for something to steal - a phone, a tablet, anything. But although the first open locker he checked had a smartphone buried under jeans and a flannel shirt, he couldn't take it.

"I can't get the stuff you want," he said after school.

"Your friends don't have anything? You can't steal an iPhone from anywhere?" She looked skeptical.

"No. What, did you steal stuff all the time before?"

She stared at him. Her dull dark eyes locked on his without a flicker of life.

"I'm sorry," he said. But he was thinking that maybe he wouldn't come visit her anymore.

"You know, you're not my only friend," she said.

"Okay."

"I see him all the time. He's a better friend than you are. He's the one who pulled me out of the earth."

"So how come he's never here? How come I haven't seen him?"

"Because he'd scare you."

"So he's ugly."

"No. He's beautiful."

Neither of them said anything. Then Lily turned on her side, turning her back to him. "It's getting dark out," she said. "You better go home. I'm sure your mommy's got dinner waiting."

***

That night he went to sleep facing his bedroom door, afraid of seeing a pale face at the window. Lily said she would go back to being dead, lifeless-dead, if she tried to cross out of the woods – or field apparently – but he didn't know if that was really true. He thought of her standing in his yard. Maybe trying the back door and walking into his kitchen, her bluish bare feet coming up the stairs. His stomach cramped with fear as he pictured his door opening and her dead eyes staring at him from the hall and with swift conviction he decided he would never visit her again.

Yet the next day in school he began to think about everything Lily had told him. About her stepfather doing things to her for months even though her mother knew and how her stepfather went out to the garage and got a brick when she said she was going to tell. It wasn't right, her mother and stepfather begging for help on the news. After school, he went straight to the woods.

He had just reached her lean-to when a dog barked behind him. He turned to see a woman in jeans and a heavy winter jacket trying to restrain a leashed German Shepard.

She called behind her, "There's a kid out here."

He turned to run for the field and two arms caught him: a bearded man in a thick flannel jacket. "Is this your tree house?" he asked. More men and another woman appeared from the trees. "Son, it's not safe to play in these woods right now. Do your parents know where you are?"

The second woman squinted at him. "I know him – he's Beth Poulson's kid," she said. "He lives in the gray house right through there. I'll take him home."

"I don't need to be walked home," Adam said.

"We want to talk to your mom, hon. You're not in trouble."

He wrenched himself free and ran. But two people from the search party rang his bell that night and his mother screamed his name with a fury he hadn't heard in years: *"Adam!"* After twenty minutes of shouting and a threat to ground him from going to Six Flags with his father next spring vacation, she decided that his aunt would pick him up after school and keep him until her shift ended.

"For how long?"

"Until they find that little girl," she snapped. "Until you show some responsibility."

Aunt Kim's green SUV was waiting for him at the curb the next afternoon.

Night after night, Adam thought of Lily walking up the path through the field and staring at his house. Sometimes he felt relieved and sometimes he felt guilty; he hated climbing into his aunt's car; but as two weeks went by, then Thanksgiving vacation passed, he was able to think less and less about Lily sitting alone on her lean-to.

"What do you want for Christmas, honey? You usually give me your list by now."

It was December now and his mother wasn't quite as anxious as she had been when Lily was first reported missing in October. An anonymous tip had placed Lily at a Nevada convenience store with a ponytailed man and a burgundy van; most of the town felt reassured that she was alive and her abductor was far. Her stepfather made a statement on the news that he felt God would bring Lily home to them for the holidays and asked everyone to keep her in their prayers.

Adam started to recite the gifts he'd planned to give Lily, then stopped. "I'll make a list on Amazon," he said.

In early December he stayed after school to watch a basketball scrimmage. He was getting a drink from the water fountain in the hall when he saw the audio-visual department's door was open; walking in, his heart began to hammer and he saw himself sitting handcuffed in the principal's office. Yet his hands operated with a mind of their own, opening desk drawers and filing cabinets to grope cables, a webcam, wireless speakers – until they closed on a tablet and keyboard in a leather folio.

He stuffed it in the side of his jacket, keeping it there through the rest of the game, the ride home, and hanging up his coat in the mud room. That night he lay awake, watching for snow. His bedroom window stayed clear and black and starless. When his mother had been in bed for more than an hour, he decided it was safe to go out.

Still in his pajamas, he slipped on his boots, retrieved the tablet and quietly opened and closed the back door. He wasn't going into the woods, just the field. He'd leave it on the big rock in the middle of the weeds. Lily would find it before it started to snow. She couldn't be mad at him now. He looked toward the woods and wondered if she could sense him, if she could see in the dark and hear long range like an animal.

The ground rustled at his feet. A rank whiff of fur and musk and deep earth filled the air and a huge shadow rose from the earth, growing taller than Lily, taller than the basketball coach at school. Adam saw golden eyes shining through the dark right before a

blinding pain slammed through his skull and exterminated the world.

***

He woke up gradually, as if sleep was a darkness that was trickling out of him to leave numbness in its place. He turned his head to the left and saw Lily's pallid face close to his.

"Merry Christmas," she said.

It took him a moment to make his arms work so he could sit up. He leaned forward. "I have to go home."

"You can't go home anymore," she said. "Oh, I got your present. Thank you."

He stood up. It was the middle of the night, he could tell by the silence of the town beyond the woods. He was in his pajamas still, but he wasn't cold. He pulled up his sleeves and saw that his skin was a bluish-white.

A wave of horror swept through him and he turned away so she wouldn't see him cry. But his throat didn't swell and his eyes stayed dry and his body hung beneath him like a marionette. "I'm going home," he said.

"I bet your mom wants you to come home," Lily said. "I bet she bought you lots of Christmas presents."

He walked to the edge of the lean-to. His mind struggled like an animal caught in a snare until his thoughts leapt to the obvious loophole. "You made it all the way down the path to my yard. I'll just stand there on the border till my mom sees me."

"You can try but he won't let it happen," Lily said. He looked back at her and she shrugged.

It started to snow, light flakes swirling down between the trees. Adam watched their descent, a ballet of dark violet against the blackness.

"Don't be mad at me," she said. "You'll like it here." "No, I won't. There's nothing to do."

"Tomorrow I'll show you where the deer sleep," she said. "I know where they all sleep. You'll know that stuff too now."

"I don't care. I'm going home."

"This is your home now." Lily tilted her head back to catch snowflakes on her upturned face. "Come sit with me and watch the snow. I like it when it snows."

***

Adam waited for Christmas morning. He thought it was Christmas at least by counting the days, though the sun rose late and the woods sank into frozen darkness early and it was hard to tell how many hours passed whenever he and Lily were pulled underground as the search parties spread through the woods with their flashlights and dogs. His name penetrated the snow and the dirt like a muted echo heard through an ocean. *Adam. Adam, can you hear us?*

Maybe it wasn't Christmas. But it was close enough. Dawn was streaking the sky over the trees and his mother was just waking up, probably, about to come downstairs and make coffee by the kitchen window overlooking the field. Lily was off tracking the deer. Adam headed up the path through the snowy field, casually at first and then he began to run. He wanted to scream for his mother but he didn't, afraid of alerting *him*, as his house came into view and he hurtled himself out of the field, out of his brief and unwanted afterlife, and into his backyard to give his mother the gift of knowledge.

The End

CASE #:51548
DEER KINGDOM
BY VALERIE ALEXANDER

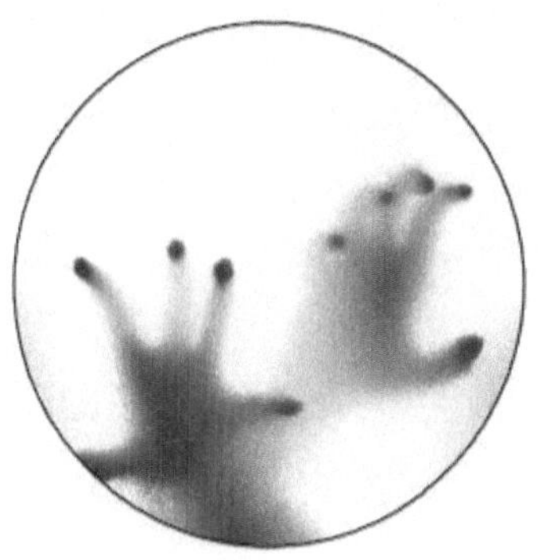

Valerie Alexander lives in Phoenix and Los Angeles. A practitioner of multiple hallowed arts such as science fiction, erotica, interstitial and horror, her work has appeared in a variety of publications, including anthologies from Cleis Press, YVLA and Lethe Press, Dark Moon Digest and other outlets. Visit her at valeriealexander.org or @vaxder.

Too Much Of A Good Thing by Katie Krantz

THE LUKE-WARM ICE CREAM CARTONS lay around Janice on the couch, their contents slowly dripping onto the mustard-yellow corduroy, turning the fabric from soft to sticky and eventually as hard as rock. There was almost every flavor and brand present. The cartons made up a rainbow that reflected against the pallor of her skin in the light of the muted TV where images of summer flickered across the screen. Sweat dampened her upper lip as she stared, eyes unblinking.

Half of her drawers were empty, half of her fridge was filled with someone else's food that would sit until it rotted, and half of her soul was torn out and thrown to the cold outside. Ice cream was the only thing that could replace his cold demeanor, and so a twenty-year-old Janice had tried to fill herself half up with it.

The floor of Janice's apartment was covered by a thin layer of trash that radiated from its center: the couch. The loudest sounds were the radiator in a dirty corner and the drip, drip, drip of a half empty carton of melting rocky road onto an empty red bag of neon orange chips, the residue of which spread across the carpet. The entire living room smelled of sweat, curdled milk, and despair.

Even in the dim light of the television, something was blooming under Janice's skin, above her stomach. It was dark and sinister, slowly spreading out under the surface. The further it spread, the thicker the glaze over her eyes became. Gradually, Janice's breathing became heavier, until every breath was like dragging a plow through quicksand. Her face turned red, then white, then purple. She tried to move a stiff hand, and her joints crushed as loudly as a bear stepping on a too thin sheet of ice over a lake. Just like the bear, her fingers slipped, the joints going every which way, the ligaments shattering like a glass thrown against the wall. The hard bones grated against each other, slipping and sliding until the skin of her hands had stretched to the shape of oven mitts.

Janice's face turned from purple back to white as she saw the blurred outline of her deformed hand through her dying eyes. She felt cold, so cold. She touched the dark blotches under her skin and slowly realized that they were the same as what stained her carpet and couch. She tried to gasp, but her deflated lungs only made the same crunching sound as her shattered hand, and suddenly she could feel it, feel all of her cells bursting from the ice crystals as her muscles turned to sludge, as her bone marrow stopped producing blood but instead produced tiny icicles of blood cells and pain, but the pain of a body-wide freezer burn was nothing compared to him leaving her.

The shards of ice that broke off from her muscles and blood slowly flowed through her body, taking their leisurely time as they pushed at her optic nerve until her vision dimmed, then slowly sawed through her spinal cord with each pump of her heart, turning her body against itself. Eventually, the tiniest particles of ice made their way past the blood-brain barrier and tore into her brain, rendering her incapable of speech, then movement, and then thought. The collection of ice in her lungs eventually pushed out the weight of one long last breath into the rancid air of her rotting apartment, minutes after her last thought had run through her head. If only she could have finished the rocky road, then it would have been worth it.

The End.

CASE #19118

TOO MUCH OF A GOOD THING
BY KATIE KRANTZ

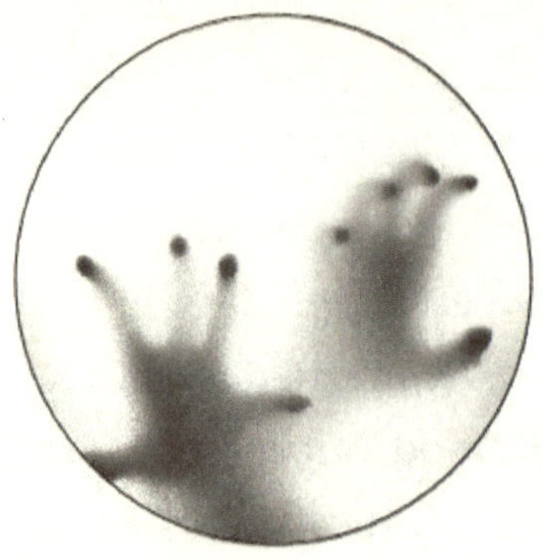

Katie Krantz is a freelance writer, journalist and student. Katie publishes for the periodical The Onlion as a regular contributor, as well as TeenInk. She loves extreme hyperbole, cats, and peppermint. Katie lives in Atlanta, Georgia, and is currently attempting to visit every vintage shop in the city.

Jonathan Apples by Dan Fields

UNTIL THE DAY I TOOK CECILY FOR MY WIFE, I never suspected that I might be a wicked man. I did love her. I know that I must have. Her sweetness, piety and affection, in short her very decency, ought to have inspired my reverent admiration. It was just so at the beginning, yet almost from the hour of our union before God, I felt my heart assailed by base and sardonic notions. Her guileless face reminded me, above all, of how blindly we give our trust to strangers, heedless of their capacity to harm and deceive us.

Do not mistake me. Consciously I harbored no ill feeling, nor made any malevolent resolution against my beloved on our wedding day. The impressions I felt were naked and aimless, no doubt prompted by the sudden change in our lives. I had not expected to feel such mutual vulnerability in our alliance. Yoked for good or ill to a woman's fate as well as my own, I felt a shadow settle on me. It did not grieve me overmuch, but while I could almost always banish it from my mind, I would perceive its unwelcome weight in moments of calm reflection.

I had met Cecily by chance in the Neelyville post office, where the recent devastation of the Doniphan town fire had obliged me to take my business instead. Cecily had left her home several weeks before to lodge with the family of a second cousin, and to work as a postal clerk. In a town like Neelyville, talk is the main commodity and a newcomer's private history may be mined for months. I gathered from several sources that she came from some wealthy clan holed up west of Saco. If that were true, I reasoned, she would have no need of a menial situation in Neelyville. Yet once I had spoken with her with sufficient friendliness to win her confidence, she confessed that her coming south had been a defiant act, a statement of independence from the arms of her peculiar and insular family. She loved them dearly but was frequently vexed, it seemed, by their clinging attachment to a few acres of ground. She had resolved to experience the wider world, and though Neelyville seemed to me a poor start, the challenge of honest work filled a want she had long felt.

Cecily loved the outdoors, and despite her mild temper she had a measure of sweet pagan wildness that charmed me. Walking the modest acreage of my ancestral farm, on my arm and at my invitation, she praised its rustic simplicity. There were hints of poetry in her nature, and she whispered little odes to the things that delighted her, barely aware that she spoke aloud.

The first time I strolled her along the south fence in the cooling shade of the barn, she mused with a sigh, "If I had been a child raised here, I should have no troubles at all."

"I've had more of this soil on my feet than any boy," said I with a laugh, "and I was happy enough."

It was true, but I had not long known the world as a man. What hardships could I claim? There was more tenderness than grit in me, and Cecily's rapture at the humble beauty of my home appealed directly to that tenderness. I held her in shade and in sunlight almost every day after.

As happens to many suitors, I had entered Cecily's life as the solution to a great crisis. From her earliest days, a fierce and possessive affection had bound her to her people. Her education had been most esoteric, conducted solely by her close kin as far as I could tell, and she knew a great deal more from folklore and obscure mythology than from the Holy Scripture so liberally used in my own upbringing. I suspect a gypsy strain of the Old World in her recent lineage. She was sensitive and loyal to her sisters and to the memory of her high-spirited mother, but being of far milder temperament she had frequently found their fervent humors overwhelming. I have detected chronic veins of melancholy and sullenness in my own bloodline, but excessive passion is a quality alien to our kind. For our virtues and our faults we are placid Midwesterners, generation upon generation.

I began my courtship with earnest expressions of love, and with only the thinnest rumor in my ear of the fortune Cecily stood to inherit. Still, the counsel of my friends and relations, in the months leading up to the wedding, began to scrub me of certain romantic ideals to the point of resentful soreness. At the latest possible hour I realized that I had fully come of age, and a childhood of bucolic contentment was passing without ceremony into a lifetime of agrarian toil. When I beheld my heart's desire, I realized with a violent shock that not a crumb of boyhood was left to me. I had inherited the farm two years before, when my father fell to fever and my mother followed, brokenhearted, shortly after. The prolonged settlement of the estate, and the late departure of my adopted cousin to seek his own way, left me a bare few weeks of bachelor's peace before the hour consecrated for our solemn vows.

I first met my wife's three sisters about a month prior to our marriage. Her family estate was in a wild part of Madison County which I had never visited, along some feeble tributary of the Little St. Francis. The house was a low, porch-girt French colonial manor hiding like an old housecat among stands of dogwood and birch. My late father-in-law had been an enterprising sort and managed to sustain himself as a kind of modern landed gentleman. I guessed that he had speculated in lead mining, as far as contemplating a dead man's trade concerned me at all. As the new cart wheels which I had bought special for the journey crackled up a long serpentine drive, Cecily touched my right hand with her left as though moved by anxiety, then fondled the free end of the rein to make the gesture seem casual.

"I am afraid," she allowed, passing her eyes down the slope of the lawn toward the river, "that you will find us a strange tribe."

I was weary and surly from a long day's travel, but the gentle worry in her tone softened the set of my face. "Soon, love," I replied, "we shall all be one tribe."

Her silence might have been doubt and it might have been assent. I had said the words without earnest hope of their ringing true, but I hoped at least to make a civil impression on the relatives who, for better or worse, held such a place in my wife's heart.

With their parents dead long before mine, Cecily's elder sisters kept the house together. Though she had gone so many miles to escape their daily influence, she was bound by familial respect to present them with her betrothed. The one to greet us at the door was Hecuba, the second eldest, ten or twelve years senior to my intended. She had a sleek rodent's nose and a pleasant cutting wit. Of the three women whose names I would come to dread, she nonetheless remained my favorite.

Our first contact brought the whisper of foreboding between us. She greeted me warmly by name, offering a hand of spidery slenderness. I grasped it with due affability. At the instant our fingers met, her features darkened like a cloud thrown across the sun by stormy wind. Something like a curious vibration in her grasp prickled down my arm, like the effect of sudden bad news. Yet in the next moment, before I could withdraw my hand, the air between us was once again light. I assured myself that the clamminess of her palm had merely taken me by surprise. Not one suspicious glance did she pay me for the rest of the visit, thought I note that our hands never met again.

"We have been at some pains to imagine," she said in a voice of sweet feline confidence, "what sort of man our Cissy might bring home. We've made quite a game of it these last few days. What a surprise to find you so fit and handsome."

Cecily reddened, murmuring sounds of embarrassment, though I could tell the comment pleased her. Hecuba led us into a dim parlor lit by fires, which I suspect would roar even in the full warmth of spring. The aesthetic effect of conflagration seemed as vital to the room as its power to stave off chill.

As soon as I entered the house, an overwhelming spicy fragrance had assailed me. My eyes welled with tears and I coughed like a man drawing too heavily on a strong pipe. I feel sure my future sisters-in-law noted my adverse reaction. I too should have taken it as an omen. The chief cause of the sharp atmosphere was the regular burning of sage in all corners of the dwelling, which Cecily informed me had been a family practice for generations. It kept away damp and was held to ward off evil influence.

Once I had adjusted to the air, our introduction was as pleasant as might be, yet the constant murmuring of the sisters made me anxious. Whenever I entered or left a room, one of them seemed to make a quiet intonation. They continually laid soft hands on Cecily as well. These were caresses in their way, but their ritual frequency belied their tenderness. Whether it was a true act of prayer or the sharing of a private game, I perceived that existence in that house was subject to countless little superstitions. I could see how Cecily, so much more sensitive to the natural than the supernatural, had found daily life among them overwhelming.

Eurydice, who had been perhaps eight years old at Cecily's birth, had nervous restless feet, and it was her habit to hum constantly at a level almost below hearing. Though she most resembled Cecily and evidently their mother, her odd manner put me off my ease. Dorcas, the eldest, was a whiskered crone of special ugliness. Her lopsided ears protruded from thin hair lacquered into an unbecoming cage. The sour set of her mouth seldom disturbed itself with speech. From a somber oil portrait hung above the mantel, I judged that it was she who most favored the paternal side. The face and wispy side bristles better suited the portly male figure of the wealthy patriarch, coupled with a velvet waistcoat and large signet ring.

The five of us spent several days walking the grounds, which were indeed beautiful, though the sisters did not seem suited to outdoor toil beyond the maintenance of a splendid and curious herb garden adjoining the kitchen. I had a foolish fancy that sprites or beasts of the wood might come by night to keep the lawn in repair. The whole estate with its constant mildness of weather and uncommonly prolific soil had the air of an enchanted place.

The sisters kept a good kitchen and comfortable beds, though small discoveries about their home habits kept me in an anxious humor. Amid the ordinary decorations of any fine old house were strewn grotesques and fetishes of horrible appearance. Half-men and imps carved in dark wood peered from niches along the walls. There were mosaic portraits of each sister on the stairs, rendered by Hecuba with small bones and the scales of colorful fish. Above the door to each room hung the small varnished skull of an unrecognizable animal. The books I found lying in every spare corner proved equally strange, with malign symbols adorning the covers and frightening passages of occult lore within. One afternoon following our daily exercise, I was leafing through a volume titled *The Communion Of The Invisible* when the humming cadence of Eurydice startled me.

"Papa kept a splendid library for us, oh, hmm hmm, yes. He sent around the world for these pages, and spared nothing in the getting of them. Dear papa, hmm hnm, poor papa."

She snapped out a long finger to trace the margin of the page, littered with notations in various hands and inks. Not one of the previous owners had written his notes in a language I recognized. For leisure reading the sisters pressed tome after weird tome on me, each full of talismanic etchings and I knew not what runic profanities, which they thought as vital to a respectable library as Mather's *Pillars Of Salt* or a first printing of Hawthorne.

Cecily had done her best to prepare me for the eerie customs of the house, and as a guest I did my utmost not to show discomfort. Only once was I sufficiently troubled to offer comment. We two were installed, with no evident qualm over our unwed state, in a bedroom draped with rich purples and reds. I had never beheld a genuine tapestry before, yet this room was positively mummified in them. The bed was a handsome four-poster carved from Congolese wenge wood, according to Hecuba. It was indeed the strangest room one might hope to inhabit. In place of a canopy, the bed frame was twined with a heavy of python stoutness, bearing a most fascinating pattern of color. Half its length was black, fading by degrees into lovely silver that seemed familiar even in such an alien context. I saw thin skeins, some red and some exceedingly fair, woven into the primary shades. Cecily watched me for some time in silence, seeing comprehension dawn on my face as I stroked the coarse fibers.

To my shock, that cord which wound dozens of yards over the bed and the adjacent wall was woven entirely of human hair. Cecily admitted that the fair tresses were her own, which I ought to have realized in an instant. From tiny girlhood, each of the sisters had grown and added her locks, a foot every few months, to the lengthening rope begun in their grandmother's time. I thought it a ghastly idea for an heirloom and could not help admitting as much to Cecily. She did not seem offended, allowing that the spiritual significance of the custom had all but died out in the western world, but she also pointed out how wondrous I had thought it before knowing of its composition.

"I had probably better not tell you," she said with a flash of mischief, "what I was raised to believe about the barbarism of coffins and cremation."

I could not help thinking of my parents lying peacefully boxed in Redbird Hill Cemetery, or of my grandfather's ashes cast into the stream where he drowned. All through dinner I envisioned appalling things that my hosts might do with their dead, entombing them in wine cellars for more robust aging or carving their bones into fine cutlery. Once I had to suppress laughter at the thought of the patriarch, that saintly heathen whose image graced the parlor, smoking over hickory coals for fish bait.

Though I could never fault their hospitality, the sisters displayed a measured, impersonal coolness when addressing me directly. The mood grew palpable over the course of our stay, until I was desperate to breathe the unembalmed air of my farm once more. Cecily was a free woman of consenting age, but I knew the purpose for our visit had been to present me and obtain some degree of approval. In the absence of outright ill treatment, I could not but feel that certain details of our accommodation had been fixed expressly to frighten or even hex me. At best they seemed reticent to bless our imminent union in any fashion I could recognize.

On the final night of our stay, however, the three sisters gave us a concert in the parlor. As Cecily and I sat placid and full in the firelight, our hostesses produced curious instruments from a chest before the hearth. Hecuba plucked strings on a long-necked mandolin. Eurydice tapped finger bells and beat a timbrel dressed with rawhide across her jittering knees. Dorcas drew a box fitted with nested glass vessels on a spindle. I recognized it from an old schoolbook of my mother's as an invention of the venerable Mr. Franklin. She moistened the glass with water from a ewer, having affixed a pedal whereby she could turn the device under her fingers. With these accompaniments they lifted their voices in a score of outlandish tunes.

For all their simplicity the airs were beguiling, but with occasional chord inversion that one might call positively alarming. The melodies given in the middle range by Hecuba were pretty enough at least. The parts of the others accorded in correct harmony, but the result lacked any gospel sweetness and seemed almost to mock the Christian psalmody. My mother had been a skilled congregational musician and once attempted to teach us. I had application without much aptitude, my cousin the opposite misfortune, and her piano still sits unplayed in the little sitting porch of my farmhouse.

Cecily lent her voice but scantly to the singing, yet her rapturous attitude as she listened made it plain that she had heard and loved this queer music from infancy. It gave me pardonable pause as it was the most like her sisters, and the furthest from her usual demeanor at home, that I ever saw her. Hecuba told me that the ballads were old standards of the folk tradition. I gave no argument, but remarked inwardly that her folk and my folk must come from widely divergent traditions. Such songs had never been sung to me before. One stanza which haunted me even into my dreams that night went thus:

Who's in the woodshed, what's in the fire/

Dead by the hand of a heart's desire?
Grief of the evening, morning of hope/
Whose is the neck in the hangman's rope?
Cries in the moonlight, wolves in the wild/
Whose are the shoes of a murdered child?

The ballads were not all so grim, but images of lost innocence and prowling corruption ran regularly through them. I recall another refrain they sang several times, a sort of coda to each new part. It pleased me more than the rest, but their manner of singing gave even such lines a forbidding tone.

My love is gone a wand'ring, oh/
Yet in my heart he lingers, oh/
No cold I'll fear from rain or snow/
If true my lover be

I married Cecily at the end of winter, fat and goodly right through the frost from the proceeds of a blessed harvest. The wedding purse was also generous, especially in the terms of Butler County. I wonder now, and may have wondered even then, whether those relatives who gave so freely had not meant to remind Cecily of what she would give up to be a farmer's wife. Hers was an eccentric clan, in the way only people of means or wild beasts of the field are free to be. Nonetheless, a respectable band of relatives from each side gathered to make merry over us, and parted in harmony. At the dinner, Cecily's three sisters made a gracious recital of their curious music, which all enjoyed save a maiden aunt of mine who found it disturbing and excused herself to take air. Dorcas, Eurydice and Hecuba came in turn to lay more hands and incantations on Cecily before departing for home. They offered me only the barest pleasantries, and I was well content to have it so.

Despite the dark murmurings of my breast, our marriage began in joy, and I did right by my sweet Cecily. She had plenty to eat and plenty to cook, dry firewood when it was wanted, and the freedom to keep what society she wished when no task bound us together in the various offices of man and wife. In the spirit of goodwill and magnanimity, refusing to take their generosity amiss, I spent at least a tithe of her family's bounty on presents for my new bride. From a chance piece of business with a butcher in Oxly, I acquired a gentle bay nag with enough vitality to carry Cecily about the farm. In mid-spring I planted her a little orchard of Jonathan apples. The four spindly trees took to my soil with fierce hardiness, yielding fruit of surpassing sweetness through many hard seasons that would follow.

Cecily did not adopt the role of farmer's wife with the usual romantic condescension of the privileged. She took to modest living with the same pleasure that a poor cousin of mine might show toward sudden showers of wealth. She had a few friends, mostly neighbors' wives, but generally preferred either my company or the cow's. Both it and I were docile in her presence, demanding nothing but the most basic and predictable daily attentions.

As to the value of children, she and I were in basic agreement, if not heartfelt accord. Cecily, I believe, nurtured the wish for a smiling tumbling brood at her bosom in the very name of love. I was interested in healthy offspring as the fulfillment of an ideal, from a sense of duty to my heritage. With the same end in mind, our differing attitudes did not seem so dire in a marriage newly begun.

I confess that a question of money, not of blood, began the true poisoning of my soul. My farm, perhaps engorged by joyful anticipation of its new mistress, had overtaxed itself with the generous yield of the previous harvest. An exceedingly lean year followed our marriage, beginning with a drought that spanned the most crucial planting weeks. My corn and sorghum came in as sparse as I had ever seen, and my hogs declined accordingly.

Cecily bore our diminished livelihood with grace, never making me feel that my success depended on uninterrupted good fortune. She pointed out that the remainder of last year's prosperity would be plenty to sustain us, despite my doubts. She did everything to cheer me, and when I would not be cheered she vowed to subsist in poverty as long as the downturn required.

Her love and faith ought to have restored me, but our differences in attitude formed a barrier between our hearts which only I perceived. I had not known sore want many times in my life, but there had been years of hail and flood on the farm. During the lowest times I had seen my father walk the brink of despair. Poverty and strife in moderation may strengthen, but in extremes they embitter. The hateful curse which my family had escaped for generations, the blight of ambition, had formed in me. I had no wish to abandon my land for wealth and idleness, but as I surveyed my domain my mind began to covet a thousand little comforts and refurbishments. I resolved not merely to endure as my ancestors had done, but to thrive as none of them had possessed boldness or wit enough to dream.

Now came the east wind to mock my prideful ambition. I saw the fragility of my fate creeping back into view, and it was intolerable to me. Suffering the old pangs of want would be hardship enough, but to face ruin before the eyes of my new wife I simply could not bear. Perversely, her constant encouragements only vexed me. It was true that she had left a close, airless life of seclusion, but she had also given up a life generously provided for. It was a choice I was never destined to have. Tortured by the shame and fear of what had not yet come to pass, I convinced myself that she must view the prospect of poverty as a novel turn of the plot, a romantic adventure for her new life story. The craven state of my heart would not permit me the assurance that she truly loved me more than any transitory state of comfort or plenty.

The unhappy threads of fate drew tighter one parching summer afternoon. I had fulfilled my morning chores with haphazard attention. The crops were so listless, the swine so petulant and ungrateful of my care, that I avoided undue exertion in my labors. I had traded with a neighbor for several jars of a vile home-brewed spirit. This I sipped with increasing frequency, secreting the vessels around the property so that I always had a drop near to hand. Even Cecily, the very soul of cheerful endurance, eyed me askance now and then, perceiving when I had indulged more than usual. On such evenings she left me in peace, not trying to engage me with bits of gossip or news.

I knew that my wife corresponded every few days with her sisters. Early in our marriage, there had been suggestions that they come to visit. On each occasion I remained silent. I did not pronounce them unwelcome, but Cecily accepted my reluctance to extend invitations before we had established ourselves on better footing. She did not begrudge me my pride, nor did she take exception to my obvious discomfort at the thought of playing host. When frustration and drink began to tax my spirit, she ceased all mention of her sisters, whose odd letters I had previously consented to hear with game good humor, read by Cecily in gently mocking tones. On this day, though, she greeted me with much excitement. I had already dulled myself with liquor, but I took instant notice of her animation. She clutched a letter which I recognized by the paper's antique smell and vivid watermark as one of Hecuba's.

"My darling," breathed Cecily in unmistakable joy, "I feel our fortune is turning once again."

I took the paper to study, and with her helpful additions I soon understood the state of things. I knew that prior to our marriage, Cecily had flatly declined the offer of a small allowance from her sisters. It was a well-meant gesture which I had done my best not to take as a slight, yet Cecily's refusal, demonstrating her faith in me as a provider, had filled my heart with the warmest pride. It was yet another of her virtuous gestures which, by that time irrevocable, had rotted to resentment in my breast. I would sooner have hanged than ask my relations in law for money by then, yet I felt its lack sharply. I had presumed the matter closed and forgotten. What Cecily never mentioned was that her sisters had instead placed a sum in trust for her later use, should she change her mind. I fancied it was no princely stipend, but knowing their maternal affection for her it would be generous enough.

I might have been angry with my wife for her failure to mention a reserve of funds in a period of such meager living, but in momentary joy I quite forgot myself. I embraced her, laughing heartily for the first time in weeks.

"How wonderful," I said, "with so much to do before next season." I had plans for expansion, investment, and superior systems of irrigation. "I don't imagine we'll have enough to start everything at once, but—"

The slackening of her face arrested me. The brightness left her cheek and her entire frame deflated. We had not understood each other.

"Oh, dearest," said she. "I was hoping to keep it aside for awhile. My sisters give it for our children, to provide for them and school them. I knew you'd approve. I remember."

I do not doubt that, in the warmth of courtship, I had promised the best care and schooling for my children. Naturally I would want better, more secure lives for them than I had enjoyed. Now more than ever, I saw the terrifying challenge of guaranteeing one's family any future at all. Yet had I not been strengthened by the hardships of my youth? Was it to be all softness and ease for my daughters and sons? *Surely,* whispered the unctuous voice I took for my conscience, *children are better for knowing want in early life.* This was the satanic cunning by which I had begun to reason with myself. I phrased sound moral principles in just the right way to suit my crude avaricious ends. I had never known my capacity to rationalize and wheedle until I met a person as trusting as my poor Cecily.

I foresaw the permanent deadlock of our situation. I could not borrow with impunity or moderation against the future of Cecily's children. I had grand hopes for improving the farm, which might take ten years of honest toil or three with the help of ready cash. Once I had begun, the entire balance would be as good as spent. Cecily, in her meek and sympathetic way, would no doubt give me what I asked, but would surrender each dollar with a tug of reluctance and a forlorn thought for our unborn offspring. A man of better wits than mine might have convinced her of the long-term good in putting the money to work at once. Any argument of mine would sound only petulant and selfish. There would be too much truth in my version.

"After all," she continued with tentative softness, "times have not turned so harsh for the two of us yet, have they?"

She could not have missed my chastened expression. I was ashamed to stand before her, still half-drunk, weighing these matters with the coldest reason. I tried lamely to laugh my ardor away as a joke. Drawing her to me with arms that fought not to tremble, I assured her that of course, to store our windfall away for the love of our children was the only thing to do.

I had grown well accustomed to refitting my self-loathing into contempt for the integrity of my wife's character. By that time I did so unconsciously. I strolled out to take fresh air as Cecily prepared supper. Having hoped to purge my melancholy, instead I felt a sudden rage invade me. I marched furiously out of the yard to the gate where I had tied my sturdy black mare. Without warning or any of my accustomed gentleness, I flung myself astride her and applied both heels. She set off at an alarmed trot toward the large pasture. The pigs made obsequious appeals as I passed near the sty, but what had I to spare for them? Soon, I was sure, my wife and I would live on husks and trash like the prodigal of Scripture, yet without the same assurance of redemption. I rode my mare hard as the devil, heedless of the ground or the obstacles. My one end was to banish the vile humors churning in my brain. I wanted to open my head and let corruption seep away. My mare screamed horribly as I drove her without mercy into the falling dark.

At last I recognized my destination, coming quickly into view. It was the little apple orchard, which my wife treasured above all else I had given her. The trees seemed to glow with special redness even in the poor light. I could make out the shape of every fruit on every limb. I had the hateful realization that those prolific trees endured while all else on the farm withered. I had not asked to be born a damned and corrupted thing. Had the example of my wife never encroached on this earth, I might have lived and died without ever knowing it.

As my mind swam with images of hacking and burning the wholesomeness right out of those apple trees, I felt my body lift with a jolt. I heard the clamor of hooves vanish away. I felt sure that the demon who dogged me had finally laid claim and would fly me away to feed its hideous brood on me. It did not occur to me that my horse had thrown me in desperation for her own life. I met the earth with my left elbow and proceeded to tumble several full turns like the wheel of a wagon. When my head whipped hammerlike into a fence rail, I had an uncanny impression of softness. My skull splintered the wood in two, but what I felt was my eyes and mind passing through smooth butter. I seemed to hear the single, enormous toll of a church bell before hearing and sight left me.

I had no sensation of passing into sleep or insensibility. In silence and blindness I still perceived the grass beneath me. I lay wooden and dumb, lacking the ability to move or react but fully aware of my condition. Recalling it, the only sense I cannot trust is the passage of time. It seemed that I lay this way for hours, possibly even a day, though the sequel of events indicates that only a few minutes passed. Indistinct bits of sound crept back to my ears. The night was quiet, yet soon the full range of its noises took shape. My sight made the same tentative return. All my limbs prickled, as when one lies too long upon an arm during sleep. At first I was amazed not to feel pain, but no sooner had I pulled myself to standing against the broken fence than the fist of an angry god clenched about my wounded head. Such was my agony that I could not produce an audible scream, though I nearly ruptured my throat in the spasm of trying. Instead of a cry, I vomited a burning gout of alcohol and bile. This I repeated three times before the effect faded such that I could walk. Shambling in loops and arcs like a drugged captive, I forced myself to keep the distant light of the farmhouse in view. Again my sense of time fails me, though I would have taken me some time to regain the safety of the yard. I nearly fell prostrate again, and if Cecily had found me there she would have sent for proper care from the doctor. Instead I met her just emerging from the house, worried by my absence. At the sight of me she gave a cry and rushed to my side. I must have looked better than I was, for I convinced her that the bruises were from a minor fall despite my manifest impairment. I assured her, with as much mastery as I could, that I was unwell from drink and excitement, and begged her leave to take myself to bed without supper. She consented with much warmth and relief, her earlier disappointment in me forgotten.

I awoke well before dawn, sore and very empty but not as debilitated as one might expect. Helping myself to cold meat and bread as Cecily slept, I marveled at the blow which ought to have killed me. Any likely reasons for my miraculous deliverance were lost on me. It was yet another missed escape from my present descent. Soon enough my pain returned, surprising me with blinding fits at any change or shift in the weather. Out of stubbornness and shame, I did not reveal to Cecily that I believed myself to have suffered some permanent fissure or lesion of the skull. It had fused well enough for me to live, but it was a marred shield for my poor brain. It is as good an explanation as any for my hasty deterioration. Every jolt, every small hiss of my hurt head recalled and, yes, deepened my bitterness. By the harsh clear light of my pain I fully glimpsed the creature I had become. I had not sufficient courage to show my naked greed to Cecily, brutally demanding her money for myself, yet I surely possessed the will to cheat it from her.

As I nursed my shameful self-knowledge, the sight of my wife's unsuspecting smile became a continual rebuke to me. Desperate to ease my conscience, I reasoned furiously and falsely with myself. I began to reinvent Cecily as the author of my misery, deliberately depriving us of prosperity for some wicked sense of control. At times I recognized this as delusion, but not often enough. Like a mad dog, I imagined my pain as the sum of myriad causes both internal and external, most of all my blameless wife. I ought to have seen a doctor. The stagnant blood in my head helped sour my thoughts and feelings, for I felt my nature changing in earnest. In my most delirious fantasy I should never have seen that money as a permanent solution to my worries. Above all, I loathed myself for desiring it above the future happiness of my family. In the malformed logic of my sickness, I concluded that acquiring the money by whatever means I could devise was the only sure way to cease coveting it.

I gave up drinking and showed Cecily every kindness, shielding my dark aim from her. Before long, our accustomed intimacy renewed itself. I embraced her with tenderness again, as affectionate in falsehood as I once had been in earnest. If she could have known how the sight of her aggravated the throb of my head, the way her gaze loomed before me as I slept, the beauty of her eyes turned hideous in nightmare, her heart would have wept tears of blood.

I resumed my daily labors with diligence and efficiency. Despite my apparent improvement I was no longer a loving and humble tiller of sod. I was merely a steely and well-tuned piece of farming machinery. All of it I did to distract from the furious working of my mind. A plan had taken seed in me, and the physical routines of nurturing my poor harvest helped its growing.

It takes no great imagination to see why Satan chose the serpent as his first weapon against the soul of man. When I resolved to destroy my innocent love for my own gain, it follows that I should have gone in search of a snake. Missouri has little need for creatures of venom. There are sufficient hardships and soul-sickness here to keep the human spirit in check. The exotic poisons that humble mankind in lively tropical climates have no place here, yet a farmer who knows his land can always find some deadly thing seeking shelter from the cold of night. The cottonmouth or moccasin snake, a legendary killer of the Southern riverlands, ranges in small numbers as far as my home county. This I knew, and was able to locate a specimen in a few days of searching.

I had a fair surplus of hay in my loft (would that it could have fed us as well as the horses), and at most times of year one could flush out a few crawling things with careful ministrations of the fork. I waded a short distance in, prodding cautiously before me until I perceived the wriggling of the creature as it fled deeper into the moldy, untended heap. I detected a pungent note of musk in the air, confirming that I had found the correct sort of snake.

Knowing the aggressive temper of my quarry I did not simply reach in to seize it. Sending a dog or even a pig after it would doubtless result in the death of at least one, probably both creatures. My plan was more fanciful, and not a little reckless. I kindled a small fire of green wood and leaves to produce thick smoke. This I suspended in a wire basket high above the dirt floor of the barn, a few feet under the eaves forming the upper loft. I stood close by with buckets of water, making sure that no spark could light the hay or the planks. Losing the barn would have been an unwarrantable expense.

Presently the loft was filled with choking billows. I allowed the fumes to continue for several minutes before lowering and extinguishing my flame. I had deliberately chosen a day that Cecily had gone visiting, lest she spy the smoke and run for help.

Climbing into the loft, my face muffled in a wet towel, I prodded with the wooden fork handle until I struck the soft, inert form of the snake. I prayed my sedation technique had succeeded and not simply killed it. Using my shovel and fork to work at a safe distance, I transferred the creature to a sturdy sack of new canvas. Binding the mouth of the sack with twine, I felt the horrid stirring of the thing inside. A more jarring combination of relief and revulsion I hoped never to feel again.

Even with my venomous instrument stored in the woodshed, I might have weakened to my scruples had not a dark star shone my way. My heart was already divided against itself. Despite the ill feeling I had manufactured against my dear one, I could not bring myself to do manful violence against her. Doing away with her by insidious means, I felt every bit the crawling reptile myself. Yet at every changing of the breeze my head screamed with agony, a sensation I associated with her infuriating meekness, not correctly with the appalling injury I had dealt myself by my own wrath.

Cecily fell slightly ill a day or two later. Here was the chance to put my plot into action before reason and better nature could overtake me. She was quite dizzy and unsettled in the stomach, not feverish but clearly in need of rest. I put her gently to bed with all assurances that I would see to the household. When I kissed her– the last time I kissed her – I kept my eyes tight shut, fearing that her loving gaze would break my resolve.

Scarcely had I assured myself by her slow breathing that she slept, than I retrieved my hateful parcel from the shed along with my heavy shovel. Creeping back through the house, I leaned the shovel against a wall just inside the room, then quickly shook the burlap out at the foot of the bed. Dazed by confinement, the snake would be enraged once it regained its senses. Any shifting by the sleeper should drive it to attack. I shut the two of them in the room together and attempted to busy myself with some mundane chore of the house. I found myself unequal to any productive work.

It seemed to me that long nights of guilty dread came and passed as I waited, though in truth it was scarcely more than an hour. I heard a low moan, the sound of my confused wife aroused by an unfamiliar sensation. Even in the delirium of execution, it pained me to imagine Cecily waking from the ordinary phantasms of sleep to the true nightmare I had cast upon her. By then it was more the compulsion to see a difficult task finished than any coherent notion of monetary gain that stayed me from venturing to rescue her at the final moment.

Long though I had prepared myself, I could not contain an abhorrent shudder as I heard Cecily's sighs transform into the warbling screams of a water bird. Seldom had I ever heard her speak in agitation, and when she wept it was always like the softest fall of rain. The terror and pain of her cries were alien sounds in our shared world, and for a moment I thought myself asleep and dreaming, perhaps perishing in the field where my head struck the fence weeks before. I had intended from the start to wait while the venom worked on Cecily, the way a hunter must give a wounded animal time to bleed before pursuing it, but my inertia for the first hour was strictly the consequence of blind disgust. Animation crept back into my limbs like the thawing of a hard freeze. It seemed an eon before my hand was again upon the bedroom door, pushing with caution as I peered inside.

The snake lay coiled near the foot of the bed, comforting itself with the last vestige of warmth in the blanketed body of my wife.

Cecily lay silent and still, with no power in her to flee or make entreaties to me. I saw the ashen swelling of her right cheek, which though caused by the reptile's bite, might have looked the same had I struck her poor face with all my might. Even the nature of her wound was a rebuke to me.

To my conspirator I expressed no gratitude, proving a traitor to the last. Grasping the shovel with savage energy, I saw the serpent rear in suspicion. The broad spade of its snout parted to show its sickly white mouth. Darting to match its hostile motion, I jabbed and scooped with the blade to worry its vile musky coils onto the floor. Its dangerous hiss was all the more motivation to strike with every jot of speed and energy I had. Thrusting downward, once then twice, I severed its angry head, the second stroke tearing through the last scrap of sinew. The jaws continued to snap for several seconds after the separation, while the horrid body writhed and convulsed for a shockingly long time. Thus, I thought, I had realized my crime without even so mute a witness as the viper.

No sooner had the snake ceased its motion than I felt a light touch graze the back of my knee. I shivered violently and threw my back against the wall, imagining that the death throes of my agent had summoned more of its kind. What I saw was worse. Cecily, disfigured and feeble from the effects of venom, had not yet given up the ghost. Her groan of pain was but another hiss of reproach, as cold and dire as the sound made by her killer. As she turned her whole face to me, I saw the true devastation of the poison which, though she was beyond hope of recovery, transfigured her with cruel slowness. The grey cheek was but a peripheral effect of the bite on the opposite side of her face. I should never have recognized her, swollen and dark across half her countenance to a degree worthy of a medical monograph. Only her left eye remained intact, blinking with difficulty through the blood-black crowding of tissue. Having seen me dispatch the serpent, she must have marveled that I did not rush to comfort or help her. I stood in the corner with an apprehensive grip on the shovel, watching her eyes. How craven I must have looked as I calculated my move. From that poor squinting eye came a minute trickle of blood, as much a tear of heartbreak as a symptom of her wound, which issued in like manner from the opposite nostril as I looked on.

In this way I was destined to shoulder the full cruelty of murder, which I had hoped to spare myself. The use of my scaled executioner had only compounded the abominable crime, and I felt dizzy with anguish even as I wrenched the bolster from beneath my wife's head, leaning my full weight on both elbows as I crushed it over her gasping face. I ground my teeth with exertion, sucking furiously at the taste of bile that welled in my throat. I planted my knee across one flailing arm as she fought to struggle from beneath me. I hummed through my nose, praying without words to any base principality that heard me, to any force save the righteous God of Abraham, for a swift end. Cecily found peace shortly thereafter, but against the cruel muffling of the pillow she pressed out a hoarse cry of despair, another sound unknown to me from our life together. She who had suffered my greed and derangement with compassion, who had forced herself against good sense to believe the best in me, gave one short utterance to the realization of my betrayal. Had I foreseen the possible failure of my original plan, I should have found a surer and more direct way, only to spare her the pain of admitting my faithlessness to herself.

She batted me weakly with her wrists, unable now even to close a fist in retaliation. The inward bleeding which would have finished her in hours took the last energy she had to resist my smothering bulk. When all motion ceased in her at last, I remained in my sprawl upon her and wept bitterly until long after dark.

Even after such an ordeal, Cecily chiefly bore the telling traces of a snakebite victim. Any incidental bruising of her face and arms went unnoticed by the neighbors and doctor whom I summoned in due course. The verdict of misadventure by animal attack, by man's first and most natural enemy no less, went unchallenged to the county coroner, courtesy of the selfsame post office where I had first beheld my bride. It was almost vexing that not one suspicious party took me for anything but a hard luck widower. Having both corpses as ready evidence worked all too well in my favor. To be suspected as a murderer, however casually, would have given me occasion to defend myself with convincing passion. Instead I was, in the eyes of my neighbors, merely an impotent victim of fate.

I thought myself unsuspected even when my wife's three sisters came for the burial. I had written to them myself, begging that they allow her interment in the orchard I had planted for her. My heart chided me for a hypocrite, yet it was as sincere a gesture of remorse as I could make. They expressed no objection, in return for my consent to a funeral ceremony of their choosing.

The day they arrived at my door, I composed my sleepless countenance into a warm, welcoming attitude. No sooner had Hecuba taken my hand than she collapsed wailing into the arms of her ever-attendant sisters. It touched my heart, though had I thought her stricken by anything besides grief, I might have caught the knowing looks exchanged by Eurydice and Dorcas.

While they took comfort in the modest spirits I could offer, I placed their luggage in a spare room I had made up for them. I planned to sleep in the parlor until such time as my wife had been removed from our bed. By chance, I stumbled and a small valise pitched forward to the floor, yawning open like the jaws of a trap. Out there fell a smaller leather case, something between a doctor's bag and an elegant sewing kit. Small pins or instruments rattled inside, but my curiosity about it fell away when I observed what had fallen out alongside it. A small linen sack, done up with coarse black string, lay on its side. I noted the harsh clink it had made upon landing, and through a burst seam I perceived the unmistakable glint of gold. It shames me to think what a shiver of glee ran through me. This was no traveler's purse. It must surely be, I told myself, a portion of the legacy I had so profaned my household to gain. I could not do otherwise than possess myself in patience until they should hand it over. I knew that I would have to wait until after the burial at least, yet once I had gathered the luggage together and set it right, I was hard put to contain the excitement in my steps. Besides the assurance that my monstrous work had not been wholly in vain, I felt that any gift assured me of my exoneration in their eyes. They had strange ways and I had worried about some dark intuition of theirs giving me away.

Quiet returned to the house as my sisters in law took up the mysterious funeral offices they had come to perform. I was politely asked to remove myself while they ministered to Cecily's remains. Once or twice I placed an ear to the door, detecting a continuous exchange of low whispers. I could not tell whether it was some incantation or spell, or the whispering of a conspiracy. My fear at being found out, and of having action brought against me, stirred anew. Yet more disturbing was that each time I bent to listen, their whispering seemed to cease, and each time I withdrew I heard the indistinct conversation resume.

After two or three hours, the sisters emerged and permitted me to see Cecily's body, if I so wished. Against the reproaches of my conscience I went in to her, and was shocked by the transformation. The women's ministrations had not been so much embalming as beautifying. The renewal was marvelous. My wife's skin, slackened in death, they had anointed so as to recall the glow of life. Her hair, cropped to half length for consecration to the family skein, had the bright pale sheen of butter, and had been brushed into perfect silken arrangement. Her arms crossed her bosom in a pose of ease and contentment. Most remarkable was the restoration of her cheek, so lately clotted with blood and venom, into a dimpling barely noticeable even at so close a distance. It took me a full minute's adoring, regretful gaze before I noticed the horrid black scarring ofer her pallid mouth.

Bending close, I found that Cecily's lips were stitched together with a familiar thread of black. The work was fine, but the effect quite ghastly. It marred her final beauty, despite the wondrous efforts made. Wishing to calm the leaping of my heart, I cradled her sweet head from behind in my quivering palm. I noticed then that her face, hair and skull had taken on alarming weight. I withdrew my hand rapidly, causing her head to rock back against the bolster. There came a dull jingling sound, also familiar and seeming to proceed from inside her. Out from beneath her soft neck slipped a folded parcel of linen. This third element, which I recognized as readily as the others, proved the dashing of my latest hope.

In some pagan passage ritual, which I had been reckless in allowing to take me unawares, my wife's three sisters had deposited the gift of gold I thought promised to me in the mouth and gullet of my late beloved. Whether some heresy from the Law of the Pharaoh, a Mithraic obscenity lost to time, or the perverse invention of my guests, it seemed a barbarous and profligate way to honor the dead. It was natural that I should emerge from the room shaken at the final sight of my wife, but I said nothing to express distaste or contradict their work. I feared that my jealous anger over losing the money might glow through in the heat of my objection.

The following forenoon we made our way to the orchard to bury Cecily. The cart which had borne us to her family home now drew a rough litter, fashioned with joists I had pulled from my loft. These I had joined and planed and polished to rude but respectable elegance. Her body was swathed in clean linen, covering all but her shut eyes and the cascade of hair spread in an immaculate halo by Eurydice's nimble fingers.

I confess to a final wrongdoing in my grim pageant as usher out-of-life. Once her sisters had arranged Cecily on the litter, they retired to finish their *toilettes* while I fastened thin straps of hide about the limbs and breast of my darling one. As I smoothed her swaddling one last time, the fabric slipped to reveal the sutures of permanent silence upon her lips. A rabid desire seized my hand with the force of a dog's bite. With quick action, it was yet possible that I could rescue a fistful of gold from the ungrudging mouth of my bride. As always I had my sharpened field knife in my pocket, and moving with as much furtive quiet as I could I passed the blade under the snug stitching, the slender iron perfectly dividing her lips. I drew it carefully upward, but found surprising resistance in the black thread. Feeling a chill of sweat over my brow, I pulled more sharply, doing my utmost not to disturb the repose of her head a second time. Only one stitch broke, with a bowstring pop that seemed to resound in the crisp air.

I weighed the expediency of drawing the thread out by degrees to part her jaw, but a crucial stab of conscience stayed me once I had burst the second stitch. I gave up the theft as futile, nothing more than a desperate flare of the devilish temperament not yet subdued by my shame and grief. I sent a searching glance over my shoulder toward the house. I feared that in taking so much time over Cecily I might have been observed. For an instant my eye seemed to catch a flicker of dark motion in the window, but at such a distance it was more likely a trick of cloud over sun reflected in the glass. The next instant, as I hastily covered her face, the three sisters came outside, which made the presence of one of them at a far window all but impossible.

The burial rite was subdued and fairly ordinary. Besides a few obscure murmurings and invocations, nothing strange or off-putting caught my ear. There was no renewal of the anticipated singing. They wept modestly between times, but carried out a brief and rather charming order of farewell.

As I set to the business of shoveling, they retired to prepare a final supper, as they were bound to leave the next morning. I uttered more than one prayer, giving each with feeling despite their hollow ringing against my heart. I prayed not to a Creator, nor to a Redeemer, but to the prone form of the injured angel disappearing beneath me, swallowed by the soil I had once given her out of love.

I came home to find a stew of surpassing richness prepared for me. I could hardly carry myself through the motions of washing with the smell of it in my nose. Sharing a meal with the women who tied me to my crime, despite our lack of warm feeling, eased me such that I failed to perceive the intoxicating effect of the food until well past the point of helping myself. As their faces swam hither and fro in my blackening vision, I opened my mouth to speak but found my tongue furry and slurred. Their mocking words of reply reached me as though spoken underwater, and rising to take stock of my poisoned state I lost balance and drifted to the earth with a soft shock.

In the black waters of a dream I seemed to swim for some time. No light found my eyes, but even muffled by the drug which had dosed me, the shrill strains I had missed in the burial ceremony came whirling in on me.

My love is gone a wand'ring, oh/
Yet in my heart he lingers, oh/
No cold I'll fear from rain or snow/
If true my lover be

Scarcely had the chorus faded from my ears when pain beckoned me up from the depths. A seam of fire crossed my belly, encircling a dull swollen sensation lodged in the very core of me. I thought at first I was in the final throes of the poisoning I now knew my sisters-in-law had given me. Instead of trembling back down into permanent oblivion, I rose again. Light reached my eyes in specks and spreading pools, until the hearth-lit interior of my home came clear. The firelight was colder than usual, almost purple in contrast to a normal healthy red, but the corners and shadows of my family dwelling were clear to me. Familiar yet forgotten spices filled the air. My wife's three sisters drifted in and out of view. From where I lay in the center of the floor, the room seemed more vast than I knew it to be. There was an ancient weirdness to the scene, a ritual pomp that recalled my brief stay as their guest many months before.

I attempted to speak, but instantly contorted as the pain in my guts flared outward through my limbs.

"He lives," I heard Eurydice say. She was grave, and seemed to have ceased her habitual humming.

"He lives and would speak," intoned Dorcas.

Hecuba loomed over me. "He may speak, if it does not pain him too much."

It did pain me, but I mastered it after two or three attempts. "Wh... what day is this? What time?"

The laughter of the sisters was like the curious fire they had built in my hearth, bright and crisp yet lacking warmth.

"He asks what time?" Hecuba scoffed. "Can the hour count one solitary bit? Know only that it is a crucial hour, the most important of your life."

I heard the faint rattle of a timbrel. Eurydice had picked up her instrument and shook it absently in her restless hand.

"What poison have you given me?" I demanded.

"What poison?" Hecuba shot back. "A venomous creature like you accuses us of poisoning? True, we concocted a draught to put you out of senses, but any other pain you feel was wrought by your own hand."

"Lying witch," I stammered as a wave of agony washed me.

Hecuba's indignation vanished in a stony grin of amusement.

"Oh," she sighed, "perhaps I speak too poetically. I confess our hands have been busy this night, yet if you have some thought of blaming us for your present misery, you are mistaken. We are but the agents of justice."

"Be reasonable," I gasped, "and tell me what suspicions you have against me."

The fire roared as Dorcas stoked it into new fury. The glow illuminated Hecuba's pale eyes, giving her face a demonic aspect.

"It was never a question of suspicion," said she. "When you took my hand in greeting three days ago, I knew the guilt of your heart as surely as if you had written your confession in blood."

"Foolishness," I spat. "Your parlor magic is no foundation to accuse me of some crime."

Her shadow grew immense, cast against the wall by wrathful flames.

"When we first met, the touch of your hand spoke only of fear and ambition. We were troubled on Cecily's behalf, that she should marry such a weak soul, but out of sisterly indulgence we gave no objection. We prayed to all we hold dear that our journey would find you prostrated with grief for the precious thing you have lost."

"I do grieve," said I. "I am crippled without her."

"I cannot doubt it," said Hecuba in a slightly softened tone. "If only you had known what you would lose when you first conspired to get at her money."

The muscles of my chest and stomach pulled at the burning seams that held them. My inward parts were ready to leap forth and spatter the ground like the bowels of Judas. Hecuba hissed with new hostility before I could voice a denial.

"Would it not have been easier to flatter us, to court our good graces, to invite us just once to your table no matter how false your motives? What sickness must have gripped your mind to turn your hand against our Cecily, the sweetest and silliest flower our family has sprouted for generations."

"I have been sick," I said. "I broke my head."

"We know," Dorcas boomed from the corner where she stood, an eerie sentinel. "We have the full measure of you."

"All is revealed, all is known" Eurydice half-sang, and thumped her timbrel.

"We are all of us crones and cripples," Dorcas continued, possibly quoting some strange passage of the occult, "and yet the mass of us abide, in wisdom and folly, from strength to strength."

"I took no gold," I gasped, desperate half-confession bleeding from me, "even when you left me alone with her. Three times I could have stolen it. I tried but I could not see it through. Have mercy and end my pain, I beg you."

"End your pain?" Hecuba scoffed. "End your lies, you scavenger! You predator! To steal your wife's tokens of legacy for the Life After would have been shameful, yet it would be petty and commonplace in the shadow of murder."

"I did not," I parried without strength. "I could not."

"You must have believed so, at first. Why else would you send a crawling nasty in your place, to bite and kill and mar her beauty? But you've forgotten that in your sheer murderer's gall, you laid her out on the very pillow used to finish her. There were fragments torn loose by her teeth, flecks drawn into her gullet by her dying breath."

"Faithless one," Eurydice said in a dire scriptural cadence, "against us and against the innocent spark of life you have sinned. Do you think it was only our sister you killed with your scheming?" Tough stunned by the proof of one crime, I would not stand accused of another.

"Who else do you imagine I have killed?"

Hecuba pounced. "Can you not imagine it yourself? In our preparation of Cecily's body we could not miss her condition."

"She was ill. Slightly ill. But what is that?"

"Ill? Fool, oh fool! How dare you think her ill when she was divinely touched? Blessed to carry the life for which she prayed, cursed to bear it in your name."

I could not resist the truth I heard in her voice. Unknowing, caught in the wicked frenzy of my heart, I had murdered not only my dear wife but also the child for whom she would have made any sacrifice.

I wailed, wishing I could perish from the roiling agony in my belly, and for a moment I thought some god or devil had shown me mercy. Yet it was not the physical subsidence of a broken soul or a mortally wounded body that I felt. It was the force of some living thing imprisoned in me. I had heard people speak of dread uncoiling within them, but the sensation was too keen in me for a mere literary expression. My sisters-in-law had conjured the ghost of my firstborn, a vengeful revenant to tear me from within.

Hecuba smiled, her solemnity collapsing in wicked glee. She must have read the very thought on my twisted countenance.

"We practice lost arts, farmer" said she, "but we are not necromancers. Otherwise would we be so grieved by the death of our darling one?"

Eurydice came forward, and Dorcas after her. They gathered in a triad above me, peering with scornful delight at my dismay.

"You agreed to let us bury Cecily in our family's customary way," explained Hecuba, "and the rite of expiation is a fundamental part of laying the wronged to rest. We could not bury you alongside her, as you will no doubt ask us to, without expurgation."

"What the devil do you mean?"

"Clever ways, clever ways," hummed Eurydice.

"We can but use what nature gives," thrummed the stony Dorcas. "As he snuffs the spark of life in his beloved," whispered Eurydice, "so we quicken the spark of destruction in him."

Her pronouncement fell exactly in time with a forceful thrust of the presence inside me. It shoved my flesh rudely outward, sliding among my natural guts in a familiar motion that reached backward to a dread as primal as the loss of Eden.

The nature of the judgment and sentence upon me was clear in an instant. It was my vile accomplice, a snake of the very kind I had used against my wife, which they had caught and sewn up inside me. The effect of my shifting, or the dissipation of some drug they had given it, now roused it among my entrails. I cannot express the measure of my revulsion at that moment. To feel the writhing of a live thing, to say nothing of that particular beast with its eerie sleekness, was a rare distillation of original horror. I could feel the pointed viper's head probing for escape, burrowing with frustration amid the tissues of my abdomen. I looked down at myself only once but could not bear the distortion of my flesh, coarsely joined with stitches and showing the serpent's movement like a hideous quilt thrown over it. I retched and gasped, but whether I feared its lodging in my gullet to choke us both, or whether I entertained some hope of its dying quietly before it did me further harm, I could not bring myself to scream.

Only after the snake had comprehended its plight, dealing two or three fiery bites to the inside of my stomach, did I gain courage to cry out again. My face was soon bloodless and covered in sweat, and I quivered as with unendurable cold, yet I gave voice to a litany of curses, first on myself and then on my three sisters-in-law. In answer, they joined hands and sang a dozen of their nameless airs, all in the same chilling harmony to which they had accustomed me. They demonstrated a new talent, modulating the key of each verse to correspond with the timbre of my screams. It might indeed have been called a beautiful quartet.

In their hideous rite of vengeance, they have shown themselves as devious and pitiless as any fit consort of the evil one, yet they need no devil's blessing to practice black and terrible arts. Those who are not witches may still keep terrible ways. There was never much love between us, but having visited such extremes of wickedness on one another, I dare to hope that we may find reconciliation should we meet again in some distant hell.

I have tried with many desolate pleas to move their hearts. I have begged them to slash my throat if they will not free the venomous thing inside me. I have asked them to tread upon us both. I have asked them to roll me into the fire. Finally, in fulfilment of Hecuba's scornful prediction, I have asked that having exacted their vengeance on me, they will at least have the mercy to bury me near the grave of my wife, if not beside her than at least not too great a distance away. Should they decide in a final fit of bitterness to plant me head-down, bootless, naked or cut in pieces, my desecrated bones will at least lie more peacefully for that.

How long I have lain here half-sensible, counting the spasms in my belly, I cannot guess. But who you are, come to sit and hear my confession, is the final mystery. The face and the attitude of the listener seems to change with the hour. At times I have thought I saw the sharp satisfied mouth of Hecuba, at others the witless visage of Dorcas. Once I fancied that soft rhythmic humming betrayed the presence of strange Eurydice. Yet this latest aspect, to whom I give my penitent account, fearing the final chance has truly come, I know you not at all and yet may dread you the most. Whether you have come for good or ill, I do not like the smell of you. Fool that I am, I thought that telling my sins might help drain this evil agony from me. Now I see the vanity of that hope, and do you smile to know it?

I would not claim to have loved or to have been much loved by any God of my fathers, but let all nature call me false if I do not now believe on His judgment and fear it. Against all I have deserved, I pray that it will be Cecily who sits with me at the end, and who will lead me whither it is fit for me to go. Several times this night a dream has taunted me, a feverish yearning to sit by her in a small Eden filled with sweet Jonathan apples. From her favorite tree, the smallest and most delicate of the four, she plucks a fruit of perfect shape and color. She offers it in forgiveness. To drive away this present pain I would fill myself to sickness, eating greedily of her pardon all the days of eternity.

The End.

CASE #: 15668

JONATHAN APPLES
BY DAN FIELDS

Dan Fields is a graduate of the School of Communication (Film) at Northwestern University. His short fiction has recently appeared in Beyond Borderlands and Indiana Voice Journal. He also writes movie and television criticism for his blog Fields Point Review. A native of Houston, Texas, Dan spent most of his twenties living in Chicago. Here, working odd jobs (sometimes extremely odd ones) and playing in a succession of bands, he came to love the shared and contrasting urban lore of his two home cities. Over many frosty hours spent commuting in the dark, he built on a longtime love of horror and suspense films to embrace all the wondrous terrors the literary world had to offer. Gradually, an amalgamation of devoured books began taking shape in his own stories and sketches, which continue to germinate and escape from time to time. Influences include Harlan Ellison, Clive Barker, Tana French, Joe Hill, Stephen King, Edgar Allan Poe, John Ajvide Lindqvist, and (on very zen and clear-headed days) the late Elmore Leonard. Dan currently resides in Houston with his wife. When not writing, he performs with the country rock band Polecat Rodeo.

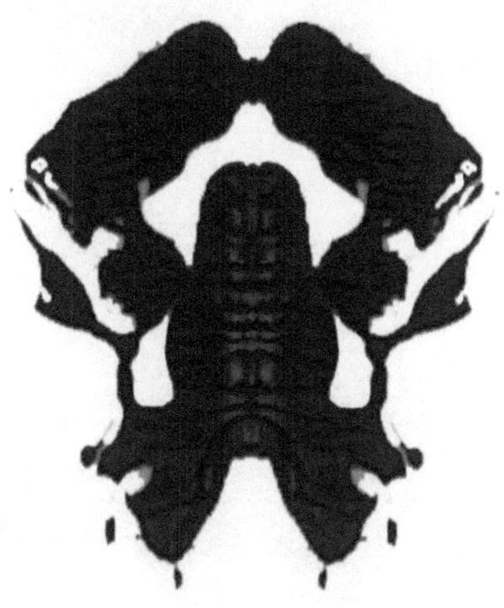

Mirrors by Jonathan Rae Rivera

Tonight,

I stare

out of windows

instead of

mirrors

and place

my palm

on the glass

      to feel

closer

to the madness.

If I adjust

my eyes

I see

myself immersed

in the flames.

The children

dance

and sing

and burn

in the street

       to feel

the fire

grow inside

so they

can learn

how to heal.

I learned how to heal

over marble

tombstones that if I

pressed my face close

enough reflected

the future.

I never   did

like mirrors.

153

*There once was a mirror in my heart that when I looked
there was nothing looking back so I broke that mirror
with one clean crunch underneath my right fist that left
knuckles dripping deep red that gathered in puddles at
my feet that reflected me but when I placed my hand to
the puddle the reflection wavered and bended and
disappeared and life went on and on and on and-*

   -*now,*

there is

nothing there

anymore.

I mopped up

the pain

and

swept up

all of the

little glass shards

that reflected

   nothing

but madness

   in my eyes.

I never did like

mirrors, so

instead I stare

out of windows to see

something else

burn

for a change.

CASE #47949

MIRRORS
BY JONATHAN RAE RIVERA

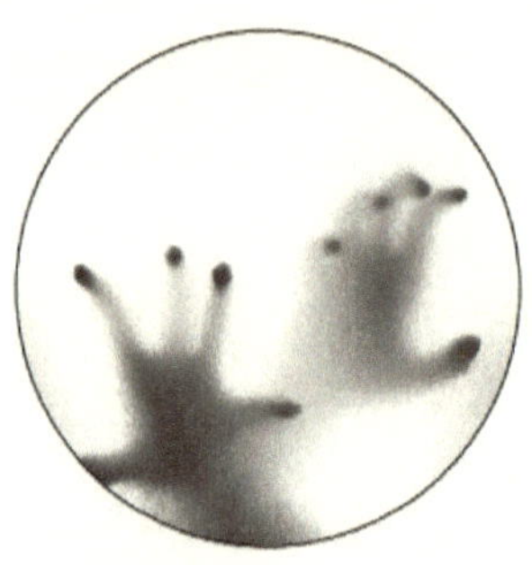

I reside in Chicago, IL. I am an aspiring writer with a BA in history from Northeastern Illinois University. I am a horror fiction writer at heart, but found a great love for poetry during my second year of college and have continued to write poetry ever since. Most of my inspiration for writing comes from my experiences growing up in Chicago. This city is my heart, yet it is one that produces so much terror and fear and tragedy that simply turning on the local news is enough to keep you awake at night. And it is that same terror and fear and tragedy that I hope resonates through all of my work.

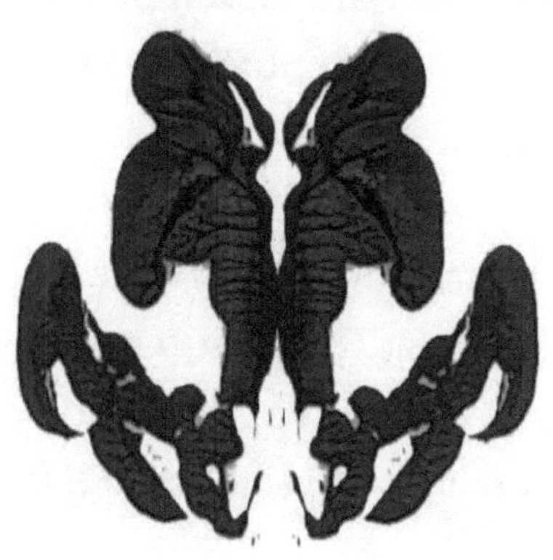

Painted In Blood by Ashley Dioses

The countess had a corpse from every home
In her high court of maiden blood and bone.
The freshest flower spurts the sweetest foam;
She savored every drop…and every moan.

No courtly daughter or shy peasant maid
Escaped her deadly pleasures and her ploys.
Their every scream was music to be swayed
From their cracked lips; their bodies were her toys.

She combed her hair with shards of pallid teeth,
And washed away, with tortured tears, the mud.
She dressed in crimson robes, and yet beneath,
Her marble skin was painted red with blood.

CASE #25667

PAINTED IN BLOOD
BY ASHLEY DIOSES

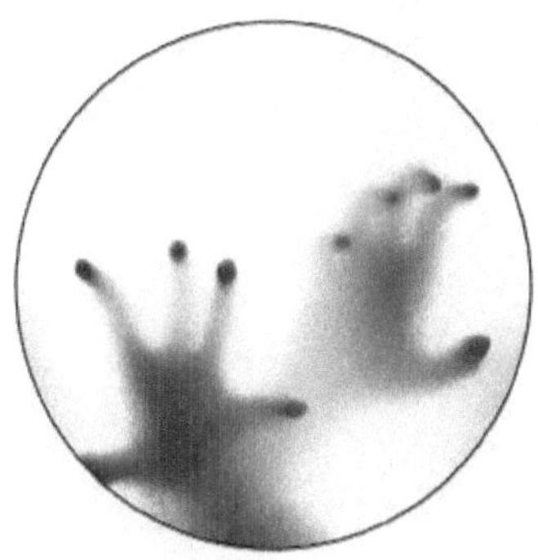

Ashley began seriously writing at the age of 12. Upon discovering the macabre work of Edgar Allan Poe, she took a borderline obsessive interest in writing horror and dark fantasy poetry and even a few fantasy novels. Her favorite authors of horror and fantasy at that time were Stephen King, Dean Koontz, J.R.R. Tolkein, Piers Anthony, and Brian Jacques.

She wrote up until her senior year of high school and then took a break before starting up again after college in 2011. With a nudge from a new friend, she discovered a new kind of horror, dark fantasy, and weird work from authors such as Clark Ashton Smith, H.P. Lovecraft, George Sterling, Donald Sidney-Fryer, and David Park Barnitz.

With this new treasure trove of horror and weird authors, she began compiling a book of poetry in the same genre to be published by Hippocampus Press in (hopefully) 2016.

Aside from writing, her other passion is martial arts. When she was 12 she started practicing a shotokan Japanese karate mix (called 'American' karate) and Judo at Red Dragon until she reached 3rd class brown belt at 15. At 18 she started practicing Soo Bahk Do, a Korean karate, where she stayed for four years, getting her black belt and taught as an instructor for a brief period of time before leaving.

On the.
Record

A Moment With Killer Party

Hi Amin and Greg and thank you for taking the time to answer a few questions about Killer Party. I suppose the best way to get started is, could you tell us a little about the project?

GREG: Killer Party is a horror-comedy musical webseries told in 13 pieces. It's about a wild college graduation party that's crashed by a masked murderer, but it's also about the hopes and fears that come with leaving friends behind and moving on to new beginnings.

So how did Killer Party come about and can you tell us a little about your backgrounds?

GREG: I was born in Arkansas and grew up really fascinated with the world wide web. I was working on websites in junior high. I loved film, but it always seemed like a far-away thing, whereas the Internet was right there. Now that I've moved to Los Angeles, it's great to be able to bring these two things together.

171

AMIN: I grew up in Casablanca, Morocco, but am half-American and devoured US culture in any way I could find it, from theater to horror films to teen comedies. Once I moved to LA for my Screenwriting MFA at USC, I was lucky enough to be roommates with Greg. We spent so much time watching and chatting about our favorite shows and movies that we figured we ought to find a productive way to justify all that time spent goofing off together… and that's how Killer Party was born.

What was your first experience within the horror genre?

GREG: I don't know if it's my first, but when I was young, I used to watch Are You Afraid of the Dark every weekend with my dad. During the week, we would buy candy at a grocery store and then eat it together. Except, one week, the episode was too scary, and it gave me nightmares, and I never wanted to watch it or anything scary again. So, as a kid, I was terrified of horror.

AMIN: It's not exactly horror, but I was both terrified by and obsessed with Beetlejuice as a 3-year-old. Looking back, it's

probably why I like my horror with humor, heart, and absurdity. My next experience was at age nine, seeing the first 10 minutes of Scream. I watched poor Drew Barrymore get slaughtered and I bolted upstairs to sleep in my parents' bed, then made my mother watch the rest of the film with me the next day. We both enjoyed it more in the daylight!

Killer Party is a slasher tale but is this your go-to choice when watching horror films?

GREG: In general, I'm a fan of horror-comedies or bad horror movies. I like some kind of ironic distance between me and the terror. That being said, my favorite horror film is The Shining, which is neither funny nor bad.

AMIN: I love slashers because I think it's neat to see creators be inventive while sticking to the formula of "hot young people get chopped up." As franchises churn out sequels, It's fascinating to see how character stereotypes change over the decades and how you can go between identifying with the victims and rooting for the killer– though I'll always be on the victims' side. Frankly, I also think the bar is lower when it comes to slashers, so it's a satisfying surprise to see them rise above it and really try to say something, like how the Nightmare on Elm Street series explores the beauty and terror of dreams.

With the writing did you split the work or was it a fully collaborative line by line affair?

GREG: We would come up with different songs that we would write on our own and then bring them to each other for notes and revisions. When writing the script, we would similarly outline the episodes, split up the episodes, write them on our own, and then bring them back to the other one, and then we'd rewrite them in the room together.

AMIN: The episodic format gave us the freedom to write things in our personal vision/tastes, because it's actually great if each episode has a slightly different tone since each is from a different character's perspective. The trick was to find common themes and plot points that bind our separate creative styles. I've also learned that collaborating isn't necessarily about each of us giving exactly 50% all the time, but rather, knowing that Greg will swoop in and do the rest when I've exhausted myself, or that I'll be there to be positive when Greg is anxious, or vice-versa (usually vice-versa!). It's kind of like we're raising a strange, evil child together.

GREG: Collaborating is definitely a lot about emotional support, organizational support, motivational support. It's not just a matter of writing the thing. You have to stay friends in the process, and you have to stay committed to seeing it through.

Was anything dropped and can you share what it was and why?

GREG: There were some dropped moments and song verses, but the big thing we cut was a subplot and two songs about two campus security guards called Bike Cop and Foot Cop.

AMIN: They functioned as a Greek chorus who would sing backup and comment on the story, and ended up in many ways being very crucial. It felt cool and unique to our setting, but ultimately, it was odd to pull so much focus from the college characters that you expect to be invested in. Once we cut the cops, it forced us to really define our main characters' relationships and led us to a much stronger story.

GREG: It also changed the killer's identity! We're sorry we killed the cops, but they had to die so our story could survive and thrive.

Is there anything that you wish you did differently?

AMIN: Everything we've done, from recording a demo CD to

staging the reading, has taught us important lessons. The only thing I wish we'd done differently is to have done it all faster! It's amazing how the anxiety that comes with rewriting or launching a Kickstarter can slow you down, and yet it all turns out fine. So from now on– less doubting, more doing!

GREG: Yeah, I completely agree. We like to wait until we're ready, but when you do that, you're never ready.

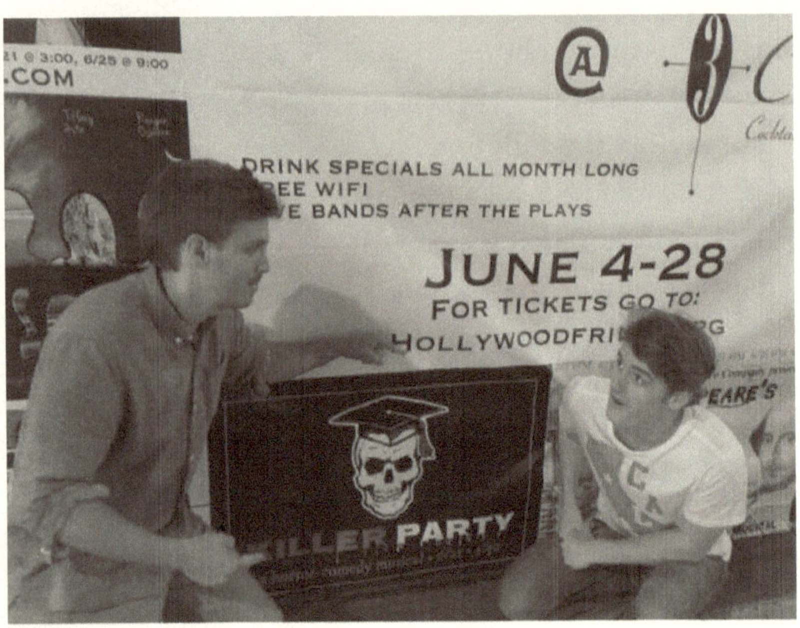

How did the cast come together for the Hollywood Fringe Festival and were they at all nervous about leaving it all out there, as it was one night only?

AMIN: We put up casting notices and had a colorful variety of LA actors audition. This was our first time running auditions like this and it was kind of terrifying to see people desperate to please us. But we found a talented cast that was also, crucially, willing to roll with a show that was still evolving as we rehearsed. We rarely had the chance to practice as a full group and our rehearsal time in the venue was very limited. So when show night came, it was so inspiring to see our actors and our amazingly talented pianist make memorable, interesting choices to overcome those limitations. We couldn't be prouder of our actors, who we're lucky enough to call friends now, too.

GREG: I think we tried to create a really low-pressure situation by not having people memorize their lines and by only doing it one night, but I think that actually contributed to the pressure of the night. It was a huge build-up to this one event, but it ultimately all turned out really well.

During the live show did you have to deal with hecklers or did you encourage call and response like The Rocky Horror Show?

GREG: We had a very respectful audience, so we didn't have to worry about hecklers. I've done shows where I want the audience to yell at the cast, but this was not one of them.

AMIN: We occasionally urged them to scream or react, and they stepped up. That's the best kind of audience– respectful, but easy with a laugh and game for anything.

Who was your favourite character and song at the Killer Party at the Hollywood Fringe?

AMIN: For me, it wasn't so much about favorites as it was about the surprise and delight of seeing moments and songs go so differently than expected or rehearsed. There's a song called "Krueger N You" about a frat bro trying to seduce a dead girl (he doesn't know she's dead, and I cannot stress that fact enough). The song isn't complex and it never really popped in rehearsal. But put that equally funny/creepy situation in front of an audience scrambling to figure out how they're supposed to feel, and combine it with two actors fully committing to the weirdness, and it resulted in the biggest laughs we got that night.

GREG: I agree. There were new things that all of the actors brought to the characters. We saw all of them in a different light, and it was a really great experience.

So moving from stage to screen, and you are telling it over 13 weeks, how long is each episode?

GREG: The typical episode is between 3 and 5 minutes, though some episodes are a little longer. The final episode is sort of a two-parter, so it's longer than the others.

Can the viewers expect new songs, characters or is it an extension of the stage show?

GREG: There will be some new surprises. We're rewriting the show based on what we learned in that reading, so anybody who saw it should expect new songs and new twists.

AMIN: Our reading was written for a cast of six in a no-frills stage show. With the web series, you'll see some new side characters and story tangents that will widen the world and really immerse you in this group of friends and their killer party.

GREG: We're going to be sharing photos and images from the
set.
We're going to be shipping out the T-shirts from the Kickstarter.
We've also got an audio show prequel that's sort of a Serial
parody that we'll put out during that time to keep interest
going. And, since some of our backers will have the opportunity
to be featured in the show as extras or victims, we think that
literal audience involvement will really help the buzz continue
to build.

Based on the outcome of the funding (which will happen I'm sure) will you be taking the show out again next year?

GREG: Thanks for your confidence! Maybe? But right now, we want to focus on filming it. One nightmare at a time.
AMIN: I hope that next year we'll be putting together the sequel! This is pretty much all I've ever wanted to do– roping loved ones and strangers into bringing my twisted fantasies to life.

If you have any feedback or would like to leave a review please head over to Amazon and share your thoughts about Sanitarium.

Thank you for your time and we salute your love for all things horror.

https://www.facebook.com/SanitariumPublishing

https://www.thesanitarium.co.uk/

https://twitter.com/sanitariumlit

https://www.instagram.com/sanitariumpublishing/